TAKEN BY THE BERSERKERS

A MENAGE SHIFTER ROMANCE

LEE SAVINO

FREE BOOK

Get a secret Berserker book, Bred by the Berserkers (only to the awesomesauce fans on Lee's email list)
Go here to get started... https://geni.us/BredBerserker

THE COMPLETE BERSERKER SAGA

For over a hundred years, the Berserker warriors have fought and killed for kings. There is but one enemy we cannot defeat: the beast within.

Remember to download your free book at www.leesavino.com

The Berserker Saga

Sold to the Berserkers
Mated to the Berserkers
Bred by the Berserkers (FREE novella only available at www.leesavino.com)
Taken by the Berserkers
Given to the Berserkers
Claimed by the Berserkers

1

The wolf stood in the center of the woodland path, lingering as if waiting for me. At first I didn't see the giant creature, mottled in shadow, with fur so black it looked almost blue. Once I did, I froze, clutching my baskets as if they could shield me. I could drop my wares and run, but if a predator of this size chased me, I was doomed.

After a good, hard glare in my direction, it slipped away, leaving me shaking with relief.

If I was wise, I'd return to the market and ask one of the villagers to escort me through the dangerous woods. Any one of the strapping young farm boys would be happy to see me home--my long, honey- blonde hair drew them like bees to nectar--but I preferred to make my way alone. My sisters and I lived at the end of the village, and I could be there before dark if no more wolves blocked my path.

A rustling in the brush told me there were more predators lurking, waiting for easy prey this close to dusk. I quickened my step and called to my sister Muriel as I drew close to our hut.

She met me on the stoop.

"Good market?"

I unslung my burden and handed her the empty baskets. "Enough to buy meat."

"Oh, Sabine, you didn't," Muriel said. "We have plenty from this month's offering."

I grunted, bending to enter the hut. I hadn't bought meat, even though I wanted to, because of the gift left on our doorstep, the gift we'd received each month since my sister Brenna had disappeared.

"How much do we have left?" I asked, waiting in the doorway until my eyes adjusted to the dank and smoke-filled space. Muriel moved by the fire, sorting the baskets and hanging up the bundles of leftover herbs.

"A whole hank. It was deer this time." Some months the meat was boar, or a slew of rabbits. It varied but it was always enough to fill our bellies for days, more if we salted and dried it. "I don't know why you don't like it."

"I'm grateful for the gift." The lie tasted bitter on my tongue. At one time, I believed the secret of Brenna's disappearance was tied to the gift of the meat. I'd waited up all night once, to try and catch the giver. Eventually, I'd fallen asleep. Just before dawn, I woke to the sound of a snapping twig. There on the ground, so close my foot could touch it, was a great boar carcass. The hunter had left it as I slept. It took all three of us to drag the beast to the firepit, and we carved it and ate on it for weeks. I never waited up to catch the the hunter again.

Muriel's voice shook me from my thoughts. "You don't have to eat it, you know. Fleur and I will eat our fair share, and give the rest away."

"Fleur should not be eating meat at all if she's still feeling ill. Just broth, and a little bit of oatcake." Youngest by a few minutes, the smaller twin took sick often. This evening, she huddled in a pile of blankets that made our bed in the corner of the hut.

I put away the herbs as Muriel pestered me with questions. "Who was at market? Did the priest bother you?"

"Nothing happened out of the ordinary. I saw a black wolf on the path coming home."

"An evil omen."

I shrugged. "No animal is truly evil. And wolves are often harbingers of good."

"Why didn't you ask one of the men from the village to walk you home? You know you could have any one of them."

I gave her a sharp look. Muriel, the eldest twin, looked far too knowing for her sixteen years.

"The men of the village are fools."

"Then how are you to marry one of them?"

"I won't. I will never marry. Love is foolish. It weakens the mind."

"What about us, then? I want to fall in love," Fleur asked in a weak voice.

I forced a smile for my two sisters. "And so you shall. You and Muriel will find your true love; I will make sure of it." I made my voice low and strong, mesmerizing as I wove the tale. "Strong men who will build you a house from the giant trees in the deep forest. They will carve your bed from a living tree and every child you bear will live."

"You don't want one then? A man?"

I bit my tongue against my true thoughts. Men were fools, too much trouble to handle. Half the time they acted like children, the other half raging brutes. I'd watched my mother fall for one who beat her and tried to grope my sister, who bore it silently, protecting us until she disappeared. My stepfather had been mauled by a beast soon after Brenna went missing. I'd laughed when I found his body.

"One man? I would never be satisfied. Perhaps two, if they were as brilliant as they were beautiful."

"Two men? At the same time?" Fleur wrinkled her nose.

"Why not?" I teased. "I can send them out together, to hunt and grunt and burp. I'll make them ask to be let back in my home."

Fleur laughed, but Muriel stayed quiet. When I puttered around the fire, she cornered me and spoke in a low voice.

"Only a few nights until full moon. Are you going to the grove?"

"Perhaps."

My sister sucked in a breath. "Be careful."

Instead of answering, I stooped and checked the unwanted meat. It came to our door fresh from the kill, bloody, as if ripped from the animal's body. Muriel roasted it with rosemary and other spices, and the smell made my mouth water. Scowling, I sliced some off for my supper.

At first I'd refused to eat the meat, as if rejecting the gift would bring my sister back. My mother had called me a fool.

"Your sister Brenna is dead," she had told me. "You have two younger sisters to care for. Any food is welcome."

I waited until my mother lay on her deathbed to tell her what I knew in my heart--somewhere, somehow, Brenna lived. I didn't know how I knew, but I did.

My mother had sighed. "Fey. Like your grandmother. She had a magic of the earth. It told her things; she knew they were true but could not explain why." My mother had clutched my hand with her wasted one. "Be careful, Sabine. Your grandmother's knowledge didn't save her when they burned her on a pyre."

"Sabine, did you hear me?" Muriel asked, bending her head close to mine so Fleur could not hear. "There's a dangerous beast about. It may be the wolf you saw. Father Benton went out one night for vespers and found all his goats slaughtered."

Last time Father Benton had spoken to me, he accused me of dallying with the devil. "How awful. The poor goats."

Muriel frowned at me. Dark-haired with grey eyes, she was growing into a beauty, but she had just as much wit, when her sweetness didn't stop her from using it. I kept her home as much as I could to keep the village men from noticing her. Some men were worse than wolves.

"I'll be careful, Muriel. You know as well as I, I need to go."

Tight-lipped, Muriel studied me for a moment before nodding. She understood.

I waited until she and Fleur had fallen asleep before slipping out of the hut in search of solitude.

Once a month, the heat came upon me. A curse from the goddess, my mother called it, though she didn't seem to suffer from it as intensely as I did. In my youth I would give in to the lust and find a man to sate the ache between my legs, but in the past few months I'd gone away alone, into the forest away from the village. The desire in me wasn't satisfied by a simple roll in the hay, it hungered for a man's strong arms, a tryst in a wild, secret place.

The moon rose and found me waist deep in the forest pool, wiping water on my fevered skin. I hummed a little as I swam.

I'd just left the pool and pulled on my gunna when I looked across the stream into the golden eyes of the wolf. My skirts tumbled into the water.

Foolish girl. I could hear my mother saying. *Out so late, alone.*

Slowly, I took a step back. The wolf stayed where it was. Another step, and another, and it seemed the beast would let me go. Muttering prayers to the goddess, I crept back the way I came.

I made it to the edge of the grove when I felt a wind at my back, a powerful pulse that sent shivers up my spine. Not daring to look back, I picked up my skirts and ran.

The lights of the hut danced in front of me. I burst onto the main path only to have strong arms like iron bands wrap around me.

My attacker pulled me backwards as I writhed and kicked. A hand slapped over my mouth. Panic choked in my throat. My legs thrashed the air as he dragged me back into the woods.

No, no, came my muffled shrieks as the trees crowded my vision. I lost sight of my family's hut. A few more steps and the light from the candle in the window disappeared in the gloom.

I kicked back at him as hard as I could, hoping to do some damage. The hand collaring my neck squeezed in warning.

"Sabine," the deep voice growled my name, and I went still with shock. "Be still."

"Please," I tried to beg, and when I couldn't get the word out, my arms and legs flailed in panic. The hand at my throat tightened, cutting off my scream. After few more kicks, the world receded and all went dark.

I WOKE SORE, my body aching. My eyes still closed, I started to call to Muriel to check the chickens for eggs, and my throat screamed for water. Head pounding, I reached for the herbs I kept near our bed for Fleur's sickness. Nothing.

I opened my eyes. Instead of the hut, I lay on the ground of a great cave, wrapped in a fur robe. The morning air felt cool on my face. Had I lain outside all night?

Last night's terror came flooding back. The deep voice growling my name, the hand around my throat. As I glanced around the wide mouth of the cave and the wilderness beyond, I realized my nightmare was real.

Fear shot through me and I came to my feet, lunging for the forest. My escape was cut short when my leg pulled out from under me. I looked back and saw the chain around my ankle.

"No," I breathed, fingers wrenching at the heavy shackle. "No, no, no."

My attacker must have brought me to this cave in the wilderness and chained me as his prisoner. A wolf would gnaw off its foot to be free. I couldn't bring myself to do more than sit trembling on the ground.

I did not wait for long. My captor emerged from the woods, padding silently on bare feet. I rose, gripping the robe around me.

In the morning light his face was just as fearsome as last night, rawboned and cruel, sharp as a blade, rugged with stubble. He wore leather breeches but his feet and chest were bare. Twining over every inch of him--his arms, his hands, even his feet--were bluish tattoos, the markings of an ancient tribe far from Alba.

My heart pounded painfully as he walked closer, but he only carried his armful of firewood past me to a large fire pit surrounded by stones. When he rose, dusting his hands, his gaze met mine like a punch. My hands clenched into fists, but I refused to look away.

At last he reached down, picked up a bucket and brought it to me, setting it a few feet away--where I could reach it despite the chain.

"You must be thirsty," he rasped. "Drink."

I waited until he stepped back before forcing myself to walk forward and do as he'd ordered. The water tasted fresh. No poison, though if my captor wanted to kill me, he wouldn't have to resort to that. He stood like a warrior at the edge of battle, face blank and muscled body tensed as if ready to fight. The strength in his corded arms had dragged me forcibly from my doorstep. When I swallowed, I realized his grip had bruised my throat.

"Who are you?" I choked out. "Why am I here?"

"My name is Maddox." His voice sounded hoarse, as if he hadn't used it in many moons. Instead of answering my other question, he set his back to me and busied himself lighting a fire.

I drank another dipperful of water. My reflection looked frightened, so I schooled my features and drank slowly, glancing about for any way to escape.

"Don't try to run." Maddox said without looking up. "The woods are full of monsters." He angled his head and flashed me a smile that froze my blood. His canines looked rather sharp. "Or maybe I spread that rumor to keep everyone away."

I stood, needing the courage my height would give me. "If you don't want visitors, why am I here?"

Maddox stood and walked towards me with measured steps. My head tipped back as he loomed over me.

"You're not just a visitor." He stopped an arm's length

away. A head taller, and broader by half, he could easily overpower me. And he had. Instead of cowering, I tensed and gritted my teeth so I would stand my ground. If he wanted me here, he could deal with my defiance. If not, then I would die.

"What am I then?"

"A friend." His gaze fell to my chest, and I pulled the robe tighter so it covered the swell of my breast. Facing this tall, tattooed warrior with feral eyes, everything in me quivered.

He reached for me. I flinched, but let him brush a few golden hairs from my cheek. His face softened as his finger teased my hair.

"Friend?" I scoffed. "Do you chain up all your friends?"

His head canted to the side as he considered my question. Up close he smelled of smoke, the wild wood, and man.

Unable to keep still any longer, I stepped away. The clink of my chain seemed to rouse him.

He dropped his hand and walked towards the forest, tossing his answer over his shoulder. "Yes."

∼

Night was falling when Maddox returned. I'd spent the day in the sun, as far away from the dark cave as I could. My chain wouldn't let me reach the fire, but I'd found a rock and beaten the chain with it, trying to find a weak point that would break my bonds. After midday, I'd become frantic, scratching at the rock that fixed the chain with my fingernails until they bled.

Finally, I sat on the rock, forcing myself to breathe deeply. I was a prisoner, but my captor didn't seem to have any malice against me. He even spoke to me. Perhaps I could reason with him.

With the rest of the water, I washed the blood from my hands and wiped my face. I combed my hair with my fingers and spent a long time braiding and rebraiding it. I would not panic. I was Sabine, considered the loveliest woman in the village, and a healer of ever increasing power. My herbs were sought after by noblemen and peasants alike. I could survive this.

That did not keep my heart from tripping wildly when Maddox walked out of the woods with his silent prowl. This time he carried a large buck slung over his shoulders. A beast of that size would be difficult for an ordinary man to carry, but Maddox walked without effort to the fire.

Throat dry, I watched the tattooed warrior gut the carcass and build a spit. His long knife tore through the flesh. The violence on top of my predicament sickened me, and I looked away.

"Do not fear, Sabine." I started at the sound of his voice. "I will not hurt you."

My hand went to my throat, sore from his bruising fingers. "You already have."

"It was necessary."

I walked to the end of my chain towards him to prove I wasn't afraid. "You could've left me alone."

His golden eyes pinned me suddenly. "I need you. "

"Why?"

"I need a healer."

I took a deep breath. "Then I will examine you."

"I'm not sick. Not yet." He speared a piece of meat with his knife and held it out to me. "Hungry?"

I was, but I didn't think I could swallow anything. My

hands fought not to close into fists at his glib answer. "Why don't you just let me go?"

He didn't answer, but kept slicing off bits of meat and catching them in a bowl. Finally he approached me and held it out. "Eat, little witch. You need your strength."

The scent of food made me even more hungry. And he was right. I needed fuel to plan my escape, but the victory in his expression when I took the bowl from him made me want to fling it back in his face. He'd given me the choicest parts of the meat, and because of my hunger, it seemed the best meal of my life. Maddox grinned, watching me devour the food.

"Good?" he grunted.

"Yes." I scowled. If he expected my thanks, he'd die waiting for it.

Forcing myself to eat slower, I took small sips from the bucket in between bites. My throat felt less sore. I almost wished it still hurt, as a reminder to me to hate my captor, instead of being intrigued by him. He'd choked me to unconsciousness. I should fear this warrior, but his deep voice and clear speech made him sound like a ruler, much more civilized than the rude surroundings.

Even his movements around the campfire were graceful, efficient. He'd set more wood nearby, where he could reach it and feed the fire into a roaring blaze that kept away the chill and the flies. For a rugged warrior, he seemed too smart by half, even if his speech was slow, stilted, as guttural as the growl of a wild creature.

The small pity I had for him made me angry. He wasn't the victim. I was. "What sort of man makes his home in a cave like a animal?"

I flinched when his shadow fell across me. But he only reached for my water bucket. "I think you know, Sabine." A tremor went through me at the sound of my name I still did not dare ask how he knew it.

"A barbarian?"

"An outcast."

When he returned with more water, my full stomach lent me courage.

"There must be a mistake. You cannot possibly mean to keep me here. What can I give you?"

He studied me as if working out what to tell me. "You are gift enough."

I tugged the bear pelt tighter around me. "What are you going to do with me?"

"Keep you safe, warm, fed."

"And chained." I shook my ankle.

"For now."

I quieted at this. No chain meant I could escape. I wondered what behavior would earn my freedom. Maddox smiled as if he knew my thoughts.

"So I am your pet," I snapped.

He didn't answer, just kept that cool smile as he built up the fire. I envisioned beating it from his face while I thought of a question that would not give him another chance to toy with me.

"I don't understand. I am but a simple village girl. I have nothing. I am nothing."

"You have magic."

"I do not--"

"Do not lie to me." His smile vanished. "I will not allow it."

"I am not lying. I grow herbs and make healing tonics. Whether they work or not is up to the goddess."

"You do not know your own power."

"You've made a mistake."

"Time will tell." Bending, he picked up the boulder securing my chain as if it were a mere pebble and carried it further into the cave.

"No." I grabbed the chain and pulled to no effect. "Please. Please do not make me go in there. I want to stay in the light."

Ignoring my pleas, Maddox carried the rock into the dry cavern, dragging me with it even though I struggled with all my might. In the end, I sat on the ground in the gloom, close to allowing myself to cry. This is what defying my captor bought me. He'd moved me only a few yards into the rocky shelter, but I would've rather remained outside in the elements. Without the sun on my face, my hope drained away.

"Do not be afraid, little witch. You are safe, for now." He started for the mouth of the cave.

"Wait," I rose to my feet, voice ringing in the enclosed space. "You're leaving?" My enemy was the closest friend I had in this place.

"It's safer for you if I am not here."

After he left, I sat mute near the fire, wringing my hands. My captor had not really hurt me, even though he seemed more a beast than man. Maybe I could survive this. I had to, not just for myself, then for Muriel and Fleur. They would be wondering what had happened to me, perhaps worrying over my fate, and their own. They were only two years younger, but I had always cared for them, kept them fed, kept them safe. What would happen to them if I was long gone? If--goddess forbid--I died in this place?

"I will not die," I muttered to myself. I would live to escape, and have my revenge on the smirking warrior who dragged me to this godforsaken place.

As the sun sank behind the trees, I explored as far as the

chain would allow. Deeper in the cave there was a sandy floor, leading to a pallet covered with a mound of old and reeking fur pelts. The musty stench filled the cave, lessened by the smoke of the fire. I went back to huddle as close as I could to the blaze, grateful for the fur robe Maddox had given me. That, at least, was clean.

As the moon rose, I prayed to the goddess to keep me and my sisters safe. The sounds of the forest filled my ears, including a call from the hills faraway, wild and lovely and achingly lonely.

I fell asleep to the howling of the wolves.

I woke during sunrise and stretched from my spot curled against the rock that kept me chained. Maddox had set the bucket near me, filled with fresh water. It wasn't until after I drank and washed my face that I realized I'd had another visitor in the night. Beside the rock, near the place where I'd slept, was a giant footprint, its span bigger than my head. Not man. Wolf.

2

Maddox found me pacing restlessly in front of the fire, the chain clinking in my wake.

"I had a visitor," I told him, pointing to the print, then clenching my hand into a fist to keep it from shaking.

He came close and knelt to observe the giant wolf print. "He accepts you. A good sign."

"Good? You left me...your healer...at the mercy of a dangerous beast. Chained, unable to run. You must let me go, or give me a weapon."

"I cannot. A weapon will not make you more safe. Better that you are helpless."

"Better?" I croaked. I'd already searched the cave. There were no rocks I could lift and use as weapons, nothing I might fight with. I couldn't even reach the fire to lift a burning torch, to see my approaching doom. "It is a death sentence."

"Arming you will provoke him. If he is to be tamed, it will not be with an axe or spear."

My fists clenched. Maddox moved to add more wood to

the fire and I followed as well as I could with the chain trailing behind me. "This is not a dog that can be tamed. This is a wolf, a wild dangerous thing." My voice echoed off the cave walls.

"And yet he is also my friend. The beast gained control several moons ago, but I believe the man in him still lives."

I swallowed. "This beast is also a man?" I'd heard of such creatures--men who could turn into wolves. I thought these were just stories told to scare unruly children from wandering too far in the woods.

Now, facing the rugged warrior who'd appeared after I twice saw a wolf, I wasn't so sure.

I worried my lip as I went to study the wolf paw. My whole hand, fingers outspread, fit into the largest imprint.

Now that I thought about it, the stories warned that the beast that gave warriors power could also overtake their minds.

"This is the one you want me to heal?"

He nodded, looking almost pleased that I now understood. I wanted to throttle him for not explaining sooner. Perhaps he thought I would not believe him unless I saw it first. "By saving him, you save many more lives. The lives of his men, his pack. The lives of your sisters and any other innocents who would fall before the beast's rage."

"But...you will not give me anything to fight him?"

"You have your wits. You have your knowledge of herbs and tonics that heal." His eyes dipped briefly to my chest, heaving under my gunna. "You have your charm, youth, and beauty."

I shook my head. "You condemn me to death."

In a blink of an eye, Maddox stood before me, a fierce look on his face. I winced when his hand came up, but his finger only traced my cheek.

"I did not stray far last night," he said. "If he had threatened you, I would've killed him. I will protect you to my last breath."

I wrenched my head away from his touch. "You chained me here to bait a monster."

He dropped his hand. "Yes," he rasped. "You are bait, but not for a monster. One night and you have already brought my friend out of the darkness. You are the only one who can heal him, Sabine. And, unless you wish to unleash a beast that will lay waste to this island, you must."

∼

I sat and thought on Maddox's words while he worked around the fire. This time he spitted several fish, and gave me one to break my fast.

"Why not just kill him? You said you would protect me from this beast. Why not destroy him, then free me and my sisters? We all could live in peace, free from the monster."

"Ragnvald."

"What?"

"His name is Ragnvald." Maddox said in a hard tone. "I could've killed him many times. Once he even bared his neck to my blade and begged for it."

My heart clenched. "Why did you not let the blade fall?"

"We share a bond closer than any brother. I must try to save him."

I picked at the bones of my fish, unwilling to look my captor in the eye. He sounded calm, but the pain in his eyes spoke of hopelessness, desperation.

"If it was one of your sisters, Sabine, wouldn't you do the same?"

I wanted to hate him. I wanted to call him cruel, but the more I knew of him, the less heartless he seemed.

"I'd do anything for my sisters."

"Good." He flung his own fish bones into the fire. "Heal my friend."

~

I slept fitfully that night, lifting my head often to see if the wolf had returned. Ragnvald never came. By dawn I was exhausted, and I curled into a tight ball, praying to the goddess to help me.

When I woke and stretched, my legs felt light. Reaching down, I discovered I did not wear the chain.

Without stopping to question why, I rolled to my feet and ran for the mouth of the cave.

I reached the forest before I heard Maddox shout.

"Sabine, no!"

My legs sped faster, carrying me into the forest. Brush whipped at my face and arms, and I raced, my ears filled with my own ragged gasps.

A growl sounded behind me, and I almost shrieked in terror. *The woods are full of monsters.* Maddox's warning rang in my ears.

A dark shape darted across my path.

I changed directions, fleeing wildly, splashing into a stream and stumbling when my feet slipped on the rocks.

Maddox caught me around the waist and took us both to the ground. I fought, crying out now, my hands digging into the earth, reaching for freedom.

"Be still," my enemy grunted, and hoisted me against his hard form, my back to his front. His hand went to my throat.

"No, no." I thrashed against him. He squeezed but not

hard enough to choke me. His other arm snaked around my waist and lifted me. I clawed at the tattooed bonds.

"Let me go, please. I cannot do it. Please just let me be."

"Be still," Maddox growled and my spine turned liquid. Slowly, he twisted me in his arms so I faced him. I gasped at the fury in his golden eyes. My death was written there.

"Please," I whispered.

"Shhh," he answered, angling my head and pressing his face into my throat. We breathed together, my two shallow pants to each of his deep exhales.

I knew that whatever beast had his friend in its grip, might claim Maddox as well.

When he released me, I almost sank to the ground in relief. He caught me and wound the thick length of my hair around his hand, using it as a leash to pull me on. Half bent over, I staggered behind him, afraid that if I didn't keep my feet under me he'd drag me on anyway.

But when I finally did stumble he turned with blinding speed, caught me, and swung me up in his arms. I huddled against him, my greatest enemy, my only comfort.

Back in the cave, he laid me on my back but didn't release my leg until he'd bent the chain around my ankle again. As soon as he let go, I tucked my knees to my chest and hid my face in them. Curled into a ball, I let my tears fall.

When I raised my head, Maddox knelt before me. The light in his eyes had dimmed. He didn't look angry, just...sad.

Somehow his disappointment was harder for me to face.

"I had to try. I had to," I hiccupped, not sure why I had to explain.

He didn't respond.

"Please, please say something."

He reached for me and I flinched, but he only lifted my leg. Cradling my foot in his lap, he took a rag from the nearby bucket and washed my leg clean of mud and leaves. I noticed the cuts on my arms and the bottom of my feet as he cleaned them and dressed them with salve.

"I'm sorry," his voice rasped like he hadn't used it in an age. "My control...slipped."

Fear brought out my temper. "You warned me of monsters. I should've guessed you are the greatest of them all. You and your...friend in the cave."

Ignoring his hurt silence, I jerked my limbs away. He was still the enemy. I had to remember that.

Maddox laid out a pelt for my scratched legs to rest on, and set a fresh bucket of water near me.

"Why do you pretend to care?"

"You are our last hope."

I bowed my head again, unwilling to look at him any longer. The censure in his words was a slap in the face.

When he knelt to finish the bandages, I pushed away from him.

"Don't touch me. I hate you." I sounded like a petulant child.

"Hate me all you want," Maddox's deep voice sounded clearer. "You are not leaving." His hand fell on the shackle. "Your freedom is not worth my friend's life."

I snorted.

"If you are a healer, you made a vow. Or do you only heal the worthy?"

Shocked he would even know of the oath I took, I shook my head. "I would heal even my greatest enemy."

I cursed myself at the triumph in his face. "But you put too much faith in my powers." What would happen when I failed? Would he snap my neck as he wanted to mere minutes ago?

His expression grew more tender. He caught my chin and heat leapt between me and his body. My heart thudded faster. "I trust you."

"Not enough to free me."

"The woods are dangerous." He paused to frown at the chain, as if wondering how I got free.

"The chain was gone when I woke." Maddox had bent the iron back around my ankle like it was made of straw and not metal. What man was strong enough to do that?

Maddox sat back on his heels, fingering the chain. "Ragnvald. Playing tricks." He smiled. "You have a champion."

"Why would he free me?" The monster had come in the night and released me. I hadn't even heard him, much less felt his touch while I slept. Cold settled on my newly washed limbs, and when I shivered Maddox tucked the bear robe around my body.

"He thinks he isn't worth saving. That alone proves that he can be saved, that he's not too far gone."

∽

MADDOX STAYED CLOSE by as my body trembled out its panic. Exhausted, I lay down and tried not to dwell on my thwarted escape. Of course my captor, a hard muscled warrior in his prime, would track and catch me. I tried to forget the way his arms had felt locked against my body.

"I must go," Maddox said. "I will be back before sundown. Ragnvald is sane enough to protect you. You're safe enough in the cave."

I refused to answer. My one hope was that this Ragnvald man-wolf would free me again.

Maddox continued as if reading my thoughts. "Ragnvald will not unchain you again. Our minds are linked once more. He knows how much we need you."

I lay all day and pondered that cryptic statement. Mostly I dozed, my body shot through with the aftermath of excitement.

Maddox returned at sundown as promised, and I lay with eyes half closed, watching him. When he came close to set down a bowl of stew beside me, I rolled to my side, away from the food.

"You need to eat."

"I do not want it."

The rich smell made my stomach ache, but I didn't move. After long minutes passed, he came back to stand over me.

"Sabine."

"I can't escape, but I can refuse to eat or drink. Starve myself to spite you."

"You won't."

I propped myself up to face him. "You don't know me. You know my name, but you don't understand me."

Maddox crouched close to me. His tattoos wove a fascinating pattern, the tale of his life. One hand lifted a tendril of my hair, holding but not tugging it. He gripped the blonde strands in his hand like a dagger's hilt, a tool, his possession. "I've watched you a long time, Sabine. I know you better than you think."

Rising, I pulled my hair from his grip, leaving a few golden strands in his fist.

"Then you know my will is strong--strong enough to do as I've said."

"You will not. You will keep healthy, and you will do as I say."

"Why would I do that?"

"Because if you do not, your twin sisters will pay the price."

He rose and stepped away while fear closed like a fist around my heart. "What about my sisters? Did you touch them?"

"They are with my men," he said. "And they are safe. For now. And no harm will come to them--if you obey."

I leapt at him, straining when the chain brought me up short. "You coward. You come and take innocent girls--"

Maddox was so swift, I only realized he'd moved when I felt his hands close over my wrists, forcing them down. I fought, shrieking. I tried to kick him and nearly lost my footing because of the chain. Maddox caught me and folded me in his arms, imprisoning my quivering body against him.

"Sabine. Be still." His hand closed on the base of my skull and squeezed in warning. His grip didn't hurt, but I froze, remembering his earlier loss of control. "Good girl," he rumbled, encouraging my surrender. He held me closer. "I've got you."

All effort left my body. My spine unhinged at his words and I huddled against him.

"You need to pick your battles, little witch," he murmured in my ear. "Your sisters are warm and fed. No harm will come to them, or to you, if you obey." His arms tightened, reminding me of their strength. "You will not fight me on this. It will not go well for you."

It was over. I had lost. Despair swept through me, a cold feeling that, perversely, made me appreciate the fierce heat of my captor's hard body.

Trembling in his arms, I tried to think, but there was no way out. Brenna had looked after me and my sisters, but Brenna was gone. There was no one to save us--only me.

"Do you understand?"

"Yes."

He let go of me and I would've crumpled onto the ground if he hadn't eased me down. I sat unmoving as Maddox cleaned up the fireside. When the wood was stocked he came to stand nearby.

"All right," I whispered. "I'll do it. I'll do as you ask."

He handed me the bowl of stew, and hovered over me until I choked down as much as I could manage.

I watched the sun set with weary eyes, blinking at Maddox when he came back to the cave wrapped in a fur pelt of his own. He lay down a few feet away.

"I'll stay with you tonight. You are in no shape to try to tame the beast."

Before it grew dark, I shut my eyes, rocking and singing a lullaby I used to sing to the girls. Three times through, once for each of my sisters, and then I lay down and curled into a ball. I had to sleep. In the morning, I would allow no more pity or frightened thoughts. If I were to defeat our enemies, I had to keep my wits.

I dreamed I heard two voices speaking over me, quiet echoes that the wind carried to my ear. Maddox's deep voice, and another deeper still, and raw as if unused for many moons.

She's so small.

Aye, but spirited.

It's been a long time, brother, but there is reason to hope.

Perhaps, Maddox said. *It is up to her.*

3

"So if I tame him, you will let us go?" I asked my dark-haired captor the next day. He seemed in a playful mood, presenting my breakfast with a flourish, calling me "milady." He even brought me flowers. As if I could be charmed by a few blooms.

"Perhaps," he said with a wolfish grin. "Perhaps you will not want to go."

My glare spoke my answer. He just laughed.

I rose to my feet, cheeks ruddy with anger. "You must take me to my sisters. I want to see for myself that they are safe and well cared for."

"My men are keeping them safe. I visited them just before dawn, and I give you my word--"

"I do not care for the word of a man who's chained me in the lair of a beast. You have no honor."

His smile fled, leaving a cold look on his rawboned face.

"Tread lightly, little witch."

"Do not call me that."

He stalked forward, and the emptiness in his eyes sent

me scrambling backwards, despite my vow not to be cowed so easily.

He flicked a gaze up and down my body and I clutched the robe closer. A frightening stillness came over him, a deadly predator gazing at his quarry. He waited for me to look away first.

"That is good anger, Sabine. Use it to do your work."

When he turned away, I scrubbed useless tears from my face.

"Wait." I made my voice desperate enough for him to heed. "I may have some skill with herbs, but what does a simple village girl know of taming monsters? What must I do?"

"If I knew what to do, don't you think I would've tried it? The prophecy told of a woman who would tame the beast within."

"I don't know how to heal a hurt I don't understand. At least tell me what he is."

Seating himself across from me, he adopted the rolling tones and mannerisms of a bard. His deep voice told the tale perfectly, and I wondered if he'd spent time at court before he became a warrior.

"There once was a king called Harald Fairhair who wished to rule all of the Northern Way, now called Norway. To defeat the jarls--the earls and chieftains--he hired a witch to make his best warriors more powerful. She cursed them, and Changed them all into Berserkers--warriors who fight with mindless rage, killing everything in their path. They rush into battle wearing only animal skins, and swords and axes do not harm them. None can stand against them." Lost in the story, Maddox's eyes glowed with an unearthly light.

I swallowed, remembering the giant paw print. "So

Ragnvald and his men are Berserkers....they can turn into wolves?

"Not just a wolf. There is a third form, between wolf and man--a true monster. In this form, Ragnvald and his warriors fought and put Harald Fairhair on the throne. But that power comes with a price. The magic eats the mind, and after a while, there is nothing but rage."

He blinked once or twice, and came back into himself. "Ragnvald and his Berserker pack came to this island as mercenaries, where I came to meet them. For almost a century, the beast was pleased with the endless cycle of fighting for greedy kings, but when peace came, we learned the extent of the curse." His voice turned bitter. "We can defeat armies and lay them to waste, but the beast that makes us great warriors craves bloodshed. During the Berserker rage, we do not know friend from foe."

After a pained silence, he continued. "There is no normal life for us. The pack has strict rules to keep the rage from breaking out, but even then we have no home, no family. We cannot risk it. As our leader, Ragnvald held the pack together, but over the years his control has slipped. And when he falls..."

"The beast will take control of his mind completely, and the whole pack will lose control?"

"If you need to fear, Sabine, fear the day the beast consumes us. It will be the end of days."

A chill swept through me at his bleak tone. If this battle hardened warrior was afraid, then what hope did I have?

"But...what can I do?"

"The prophecy only spoke of bringing you here. It did not tell what you would or wouldn't do."

I hit the ground. "That does not help me. You tell me we

all might die? You kidnap my sisters to force me to help--and then...what? What am I to do?"

He shrugged.

I bit my tongue before I enraged him again, but as soon as he'd left for the day, I scraped a handful of sand from the floor of the cave and I flung the gravel in his direction. He wanted magic? I'd show him what Sabine, herb peddler from a small village, could do. When he saw how little power I actually had, he would have to free me and let me leave.

A part of me whispered that, even if I failed, he would never let me go.

Pushing that thought away, I marched to the large bed, took up the stinking pelts, and flung them as far as I could, towards the mouth of the cave. I dumped the water over the great flat rock that had served as a bed, to wash it clean. Maddox returned to me scrubbing it with a rag.

"I need my herbs. And hot water, lots of it." I raised my chin at his frown. "You want me to do my work? Give me what I ask."

After a moment's pause he bowed his head and left, returning with my pack. I hesitated before taking it, even though I was glad to see a familiar item. Seeing my personal things in Maddox's large hands made my captivity real again.

I ignored him as I took stock of all my herbs. Maddox busied himself, carrying away the dirty pelts. When he was done, I told him I needed a way to boil water, and he disappeared again.

While he was gone, I laid out herbs that I would burn to purify the air. The cave would be cleansed, not just of mold and vermin, but of evil spirits, lurking in the shadows. When Ragnvald came to me again, the cave would smell like a woman had been here. It would smell like a home.

Late in the day, Maddox returned with a giant iron pot. He set it directly on the fire, and filled it with several trips to the stream with two buckets hanging from a yoke. Not once did he complain about doing women's work.

I supposed I should be grateful for that, though I'd rather be unchained. He did move the chain's anchor closer to the fire so I could make use of the water.

By the time night fell, I'd scrubbed the dais, and Maddox had laid fresh deerskin and pelts over it. Dried sage and a few beeswax candles burned in four corners at the mouth of the cave and behind the bed. The smoke mingled with the smell of the stew Maddox made.

With all my labors, I fell asleep as soon as I'd filled my stomach.

I woke, feeling snug and warm. Maddox had bundled me in the bear rug, and laid me on the fresh bedding. Silky fur tickled my cheek. I raised my head, and went still.

At the end of the bed, a shadowy figure sat hunched facing the fire. He was long and lean, thinner than a warrior should be, but that didn't diminish the powerful frame of his body. The low light of the fire gleamed in his blond hair.

"Ragnvald?" I whispered.

He turned hollow eyes to me, deep pits that burned gold.

I swallowed my fear. "Welcome, my lord."

He stood and loomed over the bed, naked but for a ragged deerskin slung around his hips and falling to mid thigh. Ragnvald was the tallest man I'd ever seen, taller even than Maddox. His hair was pure gold, sunnier than mine, hanging in unwashed clumps that reached to his shoulders.

My heart tripped as his shadow cut across me. I waited

in silence, but he only turned and strode back into the darkness deep in the cave. A clinking sound drew my eyes to one bare ankle, and in shock I realized he also wore a chain.

∾

"You chained him." I confronted Maddox at dawn. I'd risen and refreshed the herbs, and added wood to the dying fire. The tattooed warrior arrived soon after with more wood for the fire, and though he didn't smile I could tell he approved of my work. "He came to me last night, wearing a shackle like me."

"Not like you. His chain is longer, and fixed far, far back in the cave. You have a shorter leash."

I scowled at his jesting tone.

"The metal binding him is also warded by a witch. When he exiled himself, we took every precaution to keep him from wandering during his fits and ravaging all he meets. It won't hold him forever."

Shivering, I rubbed my arms, and wondered if I would ever sleep easy in this cave again.

"Have no fear, Sabine. He grows more himself, and less dangerous, every hour you are here."

"Who was he before the Change?" I remembered the regal poise in the way Ragnvald stood, the power in his gaze when he looked at me.

"A leader. Son of a great warrior, in a long line of lords. He would have been a fine ruler, if not for the curse."

I paced back and forth, tracing my late night visitor's steps as far as my chain allowed. "Tell me about the madness."

"The wolf and man work together. But the beast is pure hunger, pure rage. And it is not easily controlled. A century or two of fighting the urge, and even the strongest man grows weary."

"How can I help?"

"You already are. I have not seen Ragnvald in man form for several moons. Two nights, and he is sitting and eating like a man."

He pointed and I realized the dishes I'd left clean were now dirty. Ragnvald had touched the stew.

"Do you think he can be saved?"

"I do not know. But if anyone can do it, it's you."

~

I PREPARED ALL DAY, and when evening fell, I was ready. The fire burned higher, the smoke sweeter from the mulberry branches we'd added. I'd fussed over the stew and added precious spices that made Maddox hum with pleasure as he tasted them. Candles burned in the corners of a wide square around the bed, and I'd strewn the bed with lavender.

"If we treat Ragnvald like a beast, perhaps he has no reason to be more," I told Maddox. "I will treat him like a man."

Lying on the bed, I waited, staring at the fire. I must have dozed, for when I woke, Ragnvald sat on a rock not twenty paces from where I slept.

Slowly, I sat up. "Good evening my lord."

As before, he did not speak, but his eyes looked less sunken and he seemed less likely to bolt. I rose, moving carefully as if the smallest tremor would disturb him. "I hope you are pleased by the changes in your home," I murmured. I took two steps and stopped, letting the firelight caress my silhouette. I'd prepared myself as carefully as the cave.

I'd bathed earlier, using the water heated on the fire after I'd sent Maddox away. The herbs in the water left my skin and hair soft and sweetly scented. I'd left off the heavy overdress, and wore only a light shift, freshly washed and scented like my body. My feet were bare and I'd left my hair unbound.

When I faced Ragnvald again, his hungry expression told me my instincts were good. This was a man used to finer things--women and lodgings and meals with the kings he turned into conquerors. Perhaps, this night, he would remember the life he'd lost.

I lowered my gaze against his searching one.

"Allow me to welcome you properly. There is food if you want to eat, mead if you want to drink. I am happy to serve you in any way you wish." I swallowed against the lump in my throat. Even I wasn't sure how much I was prepared to offer this fallen warrior.

Ragnvald still said nothing, but after a moment he stood as if waiting for me to lead him.

"First, my lord, perhaps you'd like to bathe."

A great stone tub sat next to the fire--a slab hollowed enough for a man to sit submerged to his waist. When I'd explained what I wanted, Maddox had grumbled, but he'd gone and returned with the carven stone. He didn't tell me where he'd gotten it, and I didn't ask. Watching him carry the giant slab, muscles rippling under the strain, had been an awesome sight.

"Vikings do not bathe," Maddox had complained on his seventh trip bearing buckets from the stream.

"Ragnvald left his home long ago," I had pointed out. "If he is fit to be a ruler--"

"He is, when he is well," Maddox assured me.

"Then it is time he assumed his noble role."

Maddox raised a brow, as if to say, "Here? In this cave?"

"I cannot bring him to court. So I will bring court to the cave," I replied primly. That silenced Maddox, at least for a little while. Now I would discover if our work had been in vain.

Bowing, I swept my hand out to usher him forward. "After you, Lord Ragnvald."

I hid a triumphant smile as the lean warrior went to the bath. Busying myself with the extra buckets of water, I waited until the clink of chain told me he was lowering himself into the tub. Only when he was safely submerged did I approach.

The carven stone was massive enough to fit his folded form, though one well-muscled arm lay down the side.

"If you please, I will add more hot water." I lifted the bucket and waited for his nod. The fresh water had a few sprigs of herbs in it. After I poured, he caught one and played with it while I worked up my courage to continue.

"Soapwort." I showed him the white blossoms before I crushed them in my hands and made a foam. "I will use them to clean your arms. May I touch you?"

I tried to keep my voice light and strong, and maybe I succeeded, but my words splintered in my mind. Ragnvald held my gaze in his overpowering one for a long moment; I gritted my teeth and forced myself not to look away. He nodded again, and I dropped my eyes. Still moving slowly, mimicking the gentle grace my older sister Brenna had always had, I moved closer, and touched his arm.

In a flash, his hand moved and captured my wrist, not hurting but firm enough to send a tremor through me.

"If you please, my lord, I can bathe you."

He stared through me, eyes wild. I prayed then that he would see me, a simple woman clad only in a light shift, barefoot as a slave and ready to wait upon him. Innocent. Defenseless. Without guile. I had no weapons, no way to bind him, not even a thong to draw back my hair.

"Please," I licked my lips. "I only mean to help."

His grip tightened and he pulled me closer. I went without a fight. He could snap my neck at any point, and even if I shrank away, a two-foot chase would barely delay my death. I held my breath as Ragnvald's fingers slid to shackle my forearm, and back down to bracelet my wrist. My own arm looked so fragile in his strong, fine-boned hand. He stroked the smooth skin over my pulse with surprising care, and for a moment I saw what this rank creature was--a man, ravaged by time, but starting to return to his senses.

When he let go to rest his arm on the rim of the bath, I took a deep breath and started to wash him. I gave myself over to the meditative movement, touching him. At my request he submerged himself, and came up dripping. Grime fell away under my bold ministrations. I tried to pretend he was a statue I'd been ordered to clean, but the subtle rise and fall of the warm chest under my hand made me tremble. The battle-hardened muscle would've been flawless if not for the raised ridges of old scars. I couldn't help but trace one terrible weal on his side, and imagine the great sword that had made it. Whatever enemy Ragnvald had faced that day, he'd come out a victor, and this scar was a badge of honor, proof that this time-ravaged warrior was glorious in his prime. Even now, naked and folded into the stone bath, he lounged as if used to being bathed by a servant. But for the chain, he could be a king.

I kept my gaze lowered, but I felt his drinking me in. When I leaned over the bath to wash his chest, his fingers came to trace my collarbone, dipping under the shift to stroke that sensitive bone above my breasts. When I retreated, Ragnvald's hand followed, drifting down my shoulder, exploring the line of my arm. As I worked around him, not once did his hand leave me. His elegant fingers played over my skin, stealing my focus, making my breath ragged.

I hadn't been touched like that in a long time.

In a hoarse voice, I said, "If you lean forward, I can wash your back."

He did as I asked, and as I bent, I glanced down and realized how the water had molded my clothes to my body. I'd worn only the shift to show I had no weapons, but now I realized I might as well be naked.

When the movement of my hand slowed, Ragnvald turned. I took an automatic step back, but he only took the soapwort, and started to scrub his legs. I lathered his hair, washing it thoroughly, relieved that he didn't make me see to all of him. This was a dangerous game I was playing with an unstable man. I must have been mad, offering myself up on a platter to a brutal warrior who hadn't seen a woman in a long, long time. It would be nothing for him to drag me down to the sandy cave floor, take what he wanted, and snap my neck when he was done. I was still caught in the maw of a monster, and I needed to remember it, no matter how pretty he was.

The second my fingers left his soapy hair, he submerged himself. I backed away as he rinsed briskly and rose up out of the bath. Water poured off his powerful form. I couldn't stop myself from staring at him, at all of him freshly washed and naked in his glory. My face reddened, but I reminded myself I was a bold woman. I'd lain with men, seen them bathing naked. There was no shame in this.

But my heart pounded faster as he came towards me.

"I should rinse you," I whispered. "There's more heated water, if you desire it."

The cool night air made pebbles of my nipples. Ragnvald's fingers danced at the collar of the wet drape I wore, and I stopped breathing. When he tugged apart the knot that secured the shift at my shoulders, I let the garment fall and made no move to cover myself. Heat washed through me. I was as naked as him, but he stood boldly, while I felt feminine and vulnerable.

He moved around me to take up the two cloths I'd laid out to dry him. Once he'd wrapped one drying cloth around his waist, he returned and wrapped the second around me.

"Thank you," I whispered.

Ragnvald lifted my chin and regarded me. My lips parted, waiting, wanting even, but when he bent, he angled my head so his lips only brushed my cheek.

4

Dawn's light mottled the furs when I woke surrounded by the silky pelts. My hair was damp, proof that the night with Ragnvald wasn't a dream. I'd washed him, he'd dried me and led me to bed. After the kiss, he'd tucked me in and watched over me, looking like the pale statue I'd pretended he was. I must have fallen asleep, because I didn't remember him slipping away.

As I roused, Maddox rose from his place at the fire, and came to my side. Without speaking, he pulled off my fur blanket. His gaze hardened when he saw I was naked.

"Did he-?"

"No. He barely touched me." My hand went to my throat. I didn't know why I was trembling.

Maddox saw the tremor and pulled me into his arms. I clung to him, and the fear I'd swallowed last night cracked and spilled out of me in a rush.

"You thought...he might have--"

"No. I didn't...I wouldn't let you alone if I'd thought he would do that." His hand cradled the back of my head. "I didn't bring you here to put you in danger." His voice rumbled deep in his chest, grounding me.

"I know."

"Never again. Never again," Maddox ground out. "I won't let anyone get close enough to hurt you ever again."

The night was over. I'd survived. Last night Ragnvald had crossed a threshold, moving from beast to man, madness into healing. But I had changed also, accepted what Maddox called my destiny. A new day was here, but what did it mean? What would it hold?

Suddenly I had no future, only this moment, and this virile man before me.

With hesitant fingers, I traced his features, traced the sharp jaw, stroked the hollow cheeks. Maddox held still, until I reached his lips. He nipped my fingers, and he might as well have laid his mouth straight on my mons for the way heat flooded through me.

I could only breathe his name.

"Maddox."

His mouth fell on mine. We kissed, and he moved, taking over, the pressure on my mouth driving me backwards. I fell back on the pelts under him, whimpering as one of his tattooed hands dragged down my naked body. My hips rose to his touch. He palmed my center and glanced at my face in question, but I didn't speak, didn't break the spell, just waited until his fingers brushed my lower lips and excited me. I writhed shamelessly on the pelts.

It was happening so fast, but I needed it. I had been on edge for so long I needed the warmth of another human body next to mine, even if it was my captor. I pressed myself against him, my skin desperate for his warmth like a flower for the sun. Strong fingers stroked between my legs, then hooked into my wet hole. I hitched my leg up, eyes closing, and everything in me held its breath. This was the touch I'd longed for every month, when the full moon turned my desires into a raging inferno, set on driving me to madness.

"Sabine," Maddox breathed as his fingers fucked my wet heat.

My eyes snapped open.

We were almost to a full moon. Heat. I was in heat.

I shoved Maddox away. He responded instantly, moving up and back, but instead of jumping on him, as he probably expected, I retreated.

"No," I muttered over and over. "No." Hands over my face, I huddled on the edge of the bed.

"I'm sorry," I said, and wished I hadn't when he took it as an invite to move closer. Belatedly, I remembered I was naked, and dragged a pelt around my shoulders. Risking a glance, I winced at the hurt in his eyes.

"Sabine, you have nothing to fear from me." But when he laid his hand on the pelt covering me, I flinched, and tucked myself into a smaller ball. His great form dwarfed mine. If he wanted to force me, I had no doubt who would win.

Of course, once the heat took over and my desire took over, it wouldn't even be force. I wasn't afraid of him. I was afraid of me.

"Please."

He tugged the edge of the pelt once, but not hard enough to pull it off. I gripped it tighter, and made a small sound, a plea. A shadow fell across his face and he left me.

As I'd been up most of the night, I crawled back into the pelt's warm embrace. I must have slept, legs clamped tightly together, because when I woke Maddox was gone, but another man sat on the edge the bed, facing the fire.

As I roused he turned and smiled. My breath caught.

Golden hair down to his shoulders, carven cheeks, noble brow, this was Ragnvald, but not as I first saw him. The blond warrior looked as hale as Maddox. The transformation went deeper than clean limbs and shining hair. He'd lost the shadows in the hollows of his eyes, the wan tint to his skin, and he held himself with confidence, not the hesitant movement of a wild animal on the edge of a road, observing civilization, but not a part of it. This man was every inch the ruler I'd guessed him to be.

"Good morrow, Sabine," he said in a voice not as deep as Maddox, but rich and smooth, almost kingly.

"You can speak."

His smile "I couldn't for a long time. But it seems I have remembered how."

A measured tread interrupted us. Maddox could move as quietly as a wolf stalking a rabbit, so I knew he wanted us to hear his approach. He ignored us as he built up the fire, a surly expression on his face. I didn't know if he was angry with Ragnvald or me.

After a moment watching Maddox move stiffly around the fire, Ragnvald turned and winked at me. The gentle amusement on his face shocked me.

"How did you sleep?"

"Well, my lord. And you?"

"Never better."

Shifting on the bed, he beckoned me closer. I hesitated. This man--sometimes monster--had touched me the night before, but I still felt wary around him.

With a chuckle, Ragnvald dropped his hand. "You see, brother? She rejects me too."

Maddox didn't say anything but he stopped stomping around the fire. After a moment Ragnvald joined him, and I noticed the blond's chain was gone.

"My lord," I called. Both men turned, but I focused on Ragnvald. "You're feeling better?"

"Yes. Healthy enough I no longer need the chain." The shackle lay near one of my sage bundles. Unlike mine, it had runes stamped on its surface.

"So what now? Have I earned my freedom?"

Ragnvald grimaced. "Afraid not, little *vala*. My body heals quickly, but only time will strengthen my mind. Your help is necessary." His voice deepened. "I am grateful."

I dropped my eyes as my body quickened, responding to his intimate murmur. I couldn't bear to look at the two warriors, one dark, one light, but I felt their gaze on my body like the pull of a tide. As the moon grew round the desire in me would only grow worse. During the heat, I'd have to sequester myself, or sate it.

If they kept me captive here, would I be able to keep from losing myself to desire?

Maddox came to me and knelt.

"Run if you like, little witch." With his bare hands he snapped the shackle and freed my leg. He raised his head and gave me a mocking smile. "We will enjoy chasing you."

My heart pounded and I inclined my head. "I will not run. My sisters are still with your men."

Maddox caught a blonde curl in his hand. "Is that all that keeps you here?"

"It's not the comfort of this cave," I snapped and they both laughed. "I hope you keep my sisters in better lodgings."

Smile gone, Maddox moved away. "They are safe and provided for. I give you my word."

After a grudging nod, I waited until they turned away to dress and wash my face. The men busied themselves with roasting an entire wild boar, and my stomach growled as the scent filled the cave.

Ragnvald stood and held out his hand.

"Come dine with us," he invited, as if they were knights of honor and I was their lady. The way their attention rested on me during the meal, I fluttered my hands and brushed my hair back more than necessary and told myself it was the effect of the heat in my blood.

If they noticed my flushed cheeks, they didn't comment. We spoke of benign things, such as how Maddox hunted the meat, to what herbs I'd used to make last night's stew.

"I will need to gather more," I remarked, hoping for a reprieve from the cave.

Maddox and Ragnvald exchanged glances with a pause long enough to have a conversation, though they said nothing out loud.

"We will allow you to go into the forest, as long as one of us is close," Ragnvald ruled.

"It's not safe yet for you to venture alone," Maddox said.

I let that pass without argument. One day I would be free again, and in the meantime, I would focus on the well-being of my patient. Any attention I paid Ragnvald had the pleasant result of annoying Maddox. I practically fluttered my eyelashes at the blond as I asked, "What brought you to this island?"

"Fortune," Ragnvald said after a pause, as if looking for the words. "We were mercenaries, in service to a king."

"Harald Fairhair?" I remembered from Maddox's story.

"No. He was long dead by the time the pack sailed here."

I frowned. "You are stronger than most men, yes?"

"All men," Ragnvald corrected. "And most monsters."

"Then why do you not rule this island? You have the strength and forces to do it."

"How can a man rule a country when he cannot rule himself? No, *vala*. This wilderness is the extent of my lands."

I grew quiet at that. *Outcast*, Maddox had once called himself. The price of their cursed power.

"Once I might have wanted a kingdom, but after years of battle, I only hope for a peaceful future that I can share with a mate. " Ragnvald said, and Maddox nodded. I decided to avoid the subject of their future mate. No matter how their looks stirred my blood, as soon as this was done, I was going home.

"You are Viking, but Maddox is not. How did you two meet?"

"I saved Maddox's life."

Maddox snorted, looking younger and more jovial than I'd ever seen. The transformation made me catch my breath. For a moment he looked as beautiful as Ragnvald.

"That is not how I remember it, brother."

Ragnvald inclined his head. "You tell it, then."

Maddox took on what I recognized as his bard's voice. "There was a king--"

"A buffoon," Ragnvald broke in.

"A parasite with a kingdom," Maddox smiled like it was an old joke. "He slit his brothers' throats and took their inheritances so he had money to pay you."

"After we fought for Harald, we came to this island and became soldiers of fortune," Ragnvald explained. "We didn't care who we fought for, so we fought for that maggot and conquered a few more territories."

"Until a well spoken and devastatingly handsome--"

It was Ragnvald's turn to snort.

"--mercenary strode into your camp." Maddox waggled his eyebrows.

"You stank of peat and old blood. But you had no fear. I knew you were one of us. Berserker."

"I convinced them to fight for the opposite side. Not for money, for a lark. It was a pleasure to put that parasite's head on a pike."

"Maddox was part of the pack ever since."

"Where is the pack, now?" I asked, and wished I hadn't when all laughter fled from their faces.

"Ten leagues west," Maddox supplied quietly. His brow creased, and again I wondered if Ragnvald and he had a secret language that they used in these long pauses.

The blond raised a hand.

"Out loud, brother. She may as well know."

Maddox turned to me. "Less than half are left. I keep them camped on the cliffs over the sea. When the madness takes them we drive them off to meet their fates on the rocks. The beast can survive many things, but eventually they drown."

The meat turned to ash in my mouth. These warriors were brothers in every way but blood. To live so long only to watch the curse pick them off, one by one, would be a living hell. No wonder Maddox sought to save his friend, and through him, the pack.

"Can they be helped?" I asked. "I mean...can I help them?"

"You already have. Saving the Alpha," Maddox nodded towards Ragnvald, "binds the pack together, makes it stronger."

I nodded and flushed under the warriors' regard. I'd spoken without thought about what it would take to heal an entire pack of these broken men, but Maddox was right. I was a healer and withholding my gift from those who were suffering betrayed my oath.

Ragnvald rose first. Stooping, he kissed my forehead. "Thank you, little *vala*."

"*Vala*?" he'd called me that before.

"'Witch.' Maddox is right. You have magic."

I opened my mouth to protest and his finger barred my lips. "Not as a sorceress or as most witches do. Their power requires sacrifice--human or animal. Your power is a deeper magic, natural and of the earth."

"It still requires sacrifice," said Maddox. "But a different sort."

"What sort?"

"Self sacrifice. And that is the most powerful magic of all."

Ragnvald straightened. The shadows under his eyes had returned when we spoke of the pack, and still hadn't fled. "I must bid you two farewell for the moment. I won't go far."

With slow, old steps, he retreated back into the cave.

"Forgive me," I whispered.

"There is nothing to forgive," Maddox answered. "He had to hear of the pack sooner or later. I kept him apart to protect the pack from him, but it may have made things worse." He rubbed a hand over his face.

"Why did he leave just now?"

"He seeks the comfort of his wolf, and he does not wish you to see him Change into wolf form. But he will return, if only to remain close to you. You soothe the beast." Maddox seated himself near me. "You have questions. Ask, Sabine."

"If Ragnvald had turned, what would you have done?"

"I would've tried to kill him. The shackle would've helped weaken him, but there was still a chance he would defeat me. If I knew the shackle would hold, I would've left him to die. Isolation from the pack decays our minds faster. A lone wolf is a dead wolf.'

I remembered the lone wolf on the path from the village, who'd stopped me in my tracks on my way home.

"Maddox, how did you know of me?"

"The witch who stamped the spells on the shackle told us of a race of women with healing powers. 'Spaewives', she called them. Hedge witches. No power to work spells in the traditional way, but they still have a gift."

I picked at the meat left on my plate. "And how did you know I had this gift?"

"Two reasons. We asked the witch who gave us the shackle for Ragnvald, and she told us of a family of spaewife women. Your grandmother was one, but she was destroyed, burned at the stake. We arrived too late, after your mother had taken you and your sisters and fled to the village you call home. It took some years to find you, after that. Your mother had very little power, and so the trail ran cold." He gave me a sudden, heated look. "Until, that is, you came of age. Then your scent was easy to follow."

I cleared my throat. "And once you found me? How did you know that I had the power to even attempt to heal your pack?"

"Because I watched you, Sabine. For a long, long time."

∽

I STAYED AWAKE LONG after Maddox made his bed on the cave floor, watching his painted chest rise and fall in sleep. I knew now why the tattooed warrior barely spoke to me at first. When the beast had hold of them, it was difficult for them to remember human speech. Now that we could talk freely, one question begat seven more.

Movement from the back of the cave made me jump, but it was only Ragnvald, ambling towards the fire as if he were a lord in his hall, not barefoot in the wild. He looked heartier.

"Can't sleep?" he asked.

I shrugged.

"Moon's out. Tomorrow it will be full."

I hugged my knees tighter to my chest.

Ragnvald paused at the end of my bed and he brushed a hand over the pelts. "May I?"

I nodded. The bed was large enough to fit five men; it wouldn't hurt to share a corner of it with this tall warrior. I wondered, if we lay face to face, whether I'd feel his equal, or if his muscled body would dwarf mine as easily as it did when we were both standing.

With kingly grace, the blond warrior sat as I allowed, and regarded me.

"I heard you and Maddox talking."

"How far back does the cave go?" I peered into the gloom.

"Not far. There are tunnels that extend farther, but they are dangerous." I knew he mentioned the danger so I would not be tempted to explore, so I nodded. "But I overheard in a different way. Our minds are linked, you see. With each other, and with the pack."

The pauses between Maddox and Ragnvald made more sense.

"He's a good man, Sabine," Ragnvald spoke abruptly. "He never abandoned me, even when he should have. We did all we could, but I only grew worse. In a moment of sanity, I submitted to the shackle. We hoped the runes would help, but the decline continued...I would've died. I was content to die." He paused, and his silence held a lifetime of suffering.

"I know he had acted against you--taking you from your

home, holding your sisters hostage. Maddox would never wrong you without purpose. I think you know this." We both regarded the tattooed warrior prone on the ground, his face softened with sleep. I wondered if I'd met Maddox under different circumstances, what we would be.

"I do."

Ragnvald rose and walked to my side of the bed.

"He cares for you, Sabine. We both do."

Unbidden, the image of Ragnvald naked in the bath came to my mind. Only this time, Maddox was there with us.

The blond warrior lay his hand on my neck, and I covered it with mine, startled out of my reverie. My heart tripped faster but he only pulled the fur more tightly around me.

"You have nothing to fear, Sabine. Not from us." He picked up a pelt to make his own bed on the floor. As he retreated, he added, "And no one can stand against us. You have nothing to fear, ever again."

He lay down and was soon asleep in his place. I sat awake between two warriors, fore and aft, between me and the back of the cave, and me and the great wild. Their still, strong forms ready to protect and fight for me, even in slumber.

If I ducked my head low enough, I could see the pregnant moon winking at me from her bed in the sky beyond the wide mouth of the cave. One more day, and the heat would be upon me in full force.

Ragnvald was wrong. I had everything to fear. I could face monsters, brave captivity, look death in the face. But I couldn't deny what my heart wanted, and that terrified me more than anything.

5

I woke sweating, my body suffused with heat. My hips begged shamelessly for the release I sought even in my dreams. Slipping to my feet, I found the water bucket and drank my fill, then splashed the cool liquid over my fevered skin before I even looked around for my warriors. Ragnvald and his pelt were gone, but as I stood there, Maddox came striding out of the forest carrying a string of fish.

He grew closer and stopped, regarded me. Then, in exaggerated motion, lifted his nose and sniffed the air. My cheeks grew hot when he turned his knowing smirk on me.

Instead of commenting, he went to the fire and spitted the fish.

Still clutching the bucket, I went to sit at the fire. If I was good, maybe he'd allow me to go and seek herbs today, and bathe in the stream to cool myself.

I held the bucket in front of my body so he would not see how my nipples pointed through the linen shift, but Maddox wasn't fooled. When he walked to me, I cringed, but he only held his hand out for the bucket. I relinquished it and he disappeared down the path again to fill it. Once he returned, he held it out to me.

"Thank you." I started to take the bucket but he didn't release it.

"Don't thank me yet." His voice sounded rougher. "Ask, and I'd give you what you want, and more."

I dropped my eyes but his gaze burned my cheeks. "I want nothing from you." He relinquished the bucket and retreated, but watched as I rose and went to slip on my gunna over the thin shift. The fabric was poor armor against his piercing look--and my arousal. I pressed my hands to my cheeks, hoping to cool them.

"Where is Ragnvald?"

"Hunting. I would not risk his beast coming to the surface so soon, but he seems to be more himself. He speaks highly of your powers."

"He spoke highly of you last night." I folded my arms over my chest. "He seemed to want me to forgive you. Or at least understand why you acted as you did."

"And?"

"What's done is done." I made an impatient gesture. "It turned out for the good. I am merely waiting for you to realize he's in full health, so you will allow me and my sisters to go home." I felt a brief pang of guilt--I hadn't given much thought to Muriel and Fleur's plight lately.

"Is that what you want?"

I opened my mouth. He raised a finger.

"I can smell a lie." He smirked when I turned away. "That is not all I can smell."

I whirled back. "You speak of things you do not understand, wolf."

"Really? I am not trying to hide in plain sight. You deny your body, little witch."

"I do not," I protested. "This mood is natural. It passes."

He said nothing but prowled towards me, crowding me back. My calves hit the bed and I stopped rather than lie down before him like a willing sacrifice. Close enough to kiss, Maddox dropped his head towards mine, but he only breathed in the scent of my hair.

"When we searched for a cure, we learned all we could about spaewives. They are filled with deep earth magic, good at growing herbs and healing. During the full moon a great lust comes over them and they would lie with the devil himself." His hand brushed a leaf from my shoulder, then rested there, lightly stroking.

"I don't believe it." I said, though I knew it was true.

"Believe it, witch." He smirked. "When your desire grows unbearable, you will not have to seek out a devil. You have two right here."

I jerked my shoulder out of his hand.

"I do not want you."

"No. But, in time, you will need us."

"Never." I pushed away from him, and he yanked me back.

"Do not walk away from me."

The violence in his touch sent my heart pounding, unleashed a sudden torrent between my legs. He let go of my arm as if it burned him, and I backed away quickly.

"I don't need you. I am stronger than this," I ground out.

He didn't move, as if one step forward would snap his control. "You are strong, Sabine. You need a man as strong as you. He will break your heat and make you feel all the things you are longing for."

Staring at his mouth, I wet my lips. "I long for nothing."

Long after he left, I felt his words settle in my heart and deeper, in the aching cradle of my hips. Even slipping a hand between my legs in a private moment gave me no relief. I wanted a man's body on mine, his hands brushing down my skin, claiming, worshipping. Maddox was right. All my defenses, all the reasons I'd shorn up over time--my rationale and conscious thought all fell away under the crushing need. In the grip of the moon, I would forget my vows to remain free.

~

AT DUSK, I stood toiling over the cauldron, waiting for the warriors to return. I saw nothing, heard nothing, when someone gripped my hair and jerked my head back. The pain made me still, but Maddox's scent made me relax. He nuzzled the line of my throat and I gave in to his touch.

That's it, Sabine. I heard his thoughts. *Submit to me.*

My heart pounded harder.

Give in, little witch.

His hand somehow found its way beneath my dress, found the slippery folds that screamed for his touch. I whimpered and tried to writhe away, but my lips parted, on the verge of begging for more.

Yes. Fight it, He pulled me to the bed and laid me down. *Fight your pleasure. It will be greater when it comes. It will consume you.*

"No," I breathed aloud. "No, no." But I pulled him to me, and spread my legs wide for him to lay his hot mouth on my cunt. I panted as his tongue teased me, poking into every slick crevice, finding all my secrets until I flinched with pleasure.

"Stop--" I tried to push him away, even as my hips lifted for more. Ragnvald knelt behind me and pinned my wrists by my head. My climax rose as one warrior tongue fucked me and the other held me down. A twist of my nipple, a flick of Maddox's tongue and I tensed and screamed my pleasure to the stars. Maddox remained between my legs, lazily lapping at my sensitive tissues, and I rose up again, spiraling like smoke, only to harden, shatter and crash down. Again and again until I knew no sense.

I begged them to fuck me, needing their hard bodies pressed against mine, grounding me, as if only the touch of their flesh to mine kept my soul alive.

"Yes," I cried in relief when they filled me, the delicious stretch almost painful. I danced on the sharp edge of pleasure.

"Come," Ragnvald ordered. "Come now."

I did, screaming, gnashing my teeth against an orgasm so perfect it filled me with longing and horror that I'd never feel so complete again.

At last, I floated somewhere above their bed as they kissed me. The gentle worship of their lips undid me, and I wept.

They held me, stroking my shaking limbs as we tangled on the bed, three become one.

"We pledge ourselves to you," they said. "Give us an order and we will fulfill it."

"Let me go," I begged, clutching at them. They caught my hands.

"Anything," they said, "but that..."

∽

I WOKE sweating from my dream. Moonlight lit up the cave, but I rolled to my front and buried my head in the pelts.

The heat was upon me. When I pressed my legs together, my thighs were slippery. My nipples pebbled against the bed. I bit down on the pelts and prayed I would hold out, and not break.

∽

Morning came and at first I felt relief that I woke alone. After tending the fire, I took up the bucket for more water, only to stop short when Ragnvald strode out of the forest towards me.

"I wasn't running," I stammered. "I merely wanted fresh water."

The blond warrior cocked his head as if trying to understand. I backed away, and he went still, like a wolf scenting his prey.

There was no humanity in the golden gaze.

"Ragnvald, it's me. Sabine."

Eyes bright, Ragnvald started towards me, so focused on stalking me he didn't see Maddox until the tattooed warrior caught his shoulder.

Whirling, Ragnvald snarled at him, and Maddox pounced. They tussled, and I bit my lip to hold back a scream. Taller by a head, Ragnvald fought forward, but Maddox wrenched him back, keeping his body between me and the mad Alpha.

"No," Maddox snapped. "Not her. Hurt me--anyone else. But not her."

I breathed in relief as Ragnvald straightened and seemed to remember himself. Without a word, the Viking disappeared back into the woods. Maddox followed.

They wouldn't go far, I knew. Once he disappeared, I ran for the water bucket. Stripping a cloth into rags I washed between my legs, dousing the scent away. I scrubbed until my skin was raw, and threw the rags into the fire. A few more nights and the heat would pass. At least, I hoped it would.

That night they returned with a great horned beast slung between them. I'd burned every stick of sage I had until grey smoke lay over the cave. Still, they would not meet my eyes.

We ate together in silence, and when it was done, Ragnvald left again. I felt a gust of otherworldly wind that raised my hackles, then a large grey and gold wolf trotted into the cave and lay at the foot of my bed with a sigh.

It met my eyes for a moment and I recognized the bright gold gaze. I lay back down, wondering at the words I heard inside my mind.

Forgive me.

6

From then on the warriors stayed away as much as they could. The slow waning of the moon did nothing to diminish my need. If anything, it grew.

One night, after long hours tossing restlessly on the pelts, I heard a soft movement and opened my eyes.

Both men sat on the edge of the bed, the light in their eyes beacons in the night.

I sat up. Before I'd fallen asleep I'd tried to pleasure myself, fingers rubbing fruitlessly for release only a man could bring. Even the touch of fabric on my skin was unbearable, so I'd stripped it off.

As I grew more awake, I remembered I was naked under the pelts. The way the men fixed on my bare shoulders, I knew this fact wasn't lost on them.

It didn't matter. The heat infected my mind and all my good sense. Instead of clutching the pelts to my naked chest, I let them slip away, and waited.

Ragnvald moved and Maddox followed a hairsbreadth after, both coming to stand on either side of me. At first they only touched my hair, twining and twisting it, brushing it off my shoulders, away from my vulnerable neck. As they tugged the pelt away from my naked flesh, I pressed my legs together, but the wetness leaking from me was too much to hide. I fought not to squirm under their gaze.

At last Ragnvald lifted his eyes from the shining center of my thighs.

"How long have you suffered like this?"

Maddox answered for me. "Too long."

Ragnvald wrapped a hand around my ankle. Studying my expression, he slid his hand up my calf and then over my knee and thigh.

"Please," I breathed. For years I'd loved and dreaded the full moon, its luminous pull on the desire I'd suffered in secret. It wouldn't hurt for me to give in, just once, for a little while.

Maddox came to my back, his arms securing me. I didn't fight, only watched as Ragnvald knelt between my legs. Bowing his regal head, the Alpha kissed me. His mouth tasted of honey, heat and longing. It was everything I'd been searching for my entire life, and when the kiss ended, I touched his face to make sure he was real. His large hand came to my face also, before trailing lower, sweeping over my bare chest and driving lower still. My hips were already lifting but he ignored the soft nest at the juncture of my thighs, choosing instead to stroke up and down the length of my legs, little touches designed to drive me mad.

Maddox pulled me closer, my back to his bare chest. I sank into him, and gasped when his tattooed hands cupped my breasts. My legs spread wider for Ragnvald's exploration.

"Do you know how long it's been?" Maddox rasped. I could've cried at the raw need in his voice. "Do you know how long we've waited for you?"

His grip tightened, made my breasts throb, and I understood their delicious intent. These warriors would possess me tonight, every inch.

"Do you know how long I watched and desired you?" Maddox's lips touched my ear. "Every night."

Ragnvald went on with his perfect torment, tasting me, swirling and flicking his tongue, dancing closer, drawing further away; never satisfying, but licking the fire in me hotter and flames higher and higher. He tasted every crevice, every secret place, as his hands cupped my bottom.

"How long should we make you wait? How long should we torture you as you tortured us?" Maddox kept up the sinister whisper as his clever fingers caged my breasts, gripped them, twisted the nipples until I writhed pressing further into his hands. Begging mindlessly for something, anything, and helpless to do anything but accept what they wanted to give.

Ragnvald seemed content to lounge between my thighs and let his tongue trail up the inner seam of one leg, down the other. As soon as I relaxed, he added teeth, little nips that made my hips jump and my center cream.

"Please," I choked out finally. One of Maddox's hands left my breast and encircled my neck.

"Please, what, Sabine?" The hard core of me melted when he breathed my name. "Beg for what you want, little one. We may give it to you."

"Please..."

Ragnvald's tongue did a pass closer to my weeping slit, and my hips bucked harder.

"Tell us, little witch," Maddox chuckled, then nipped my ear. I thrashed, trying to get away, but Ragnvald's hands held my legs down without his mouth giving pause. His tongue lashed my inner thighs, licking up the wetness there.

"I don't want this," I lied, even as my wanton body

leaked more of my juices for Ragvald to lap up.

"No lying." Maddox's hand tightened a little at my neck. "Lies get little ones punished. But tell the truth, and we'll give you want you want."

"I--should not want this."

"Good girl." Maddox's voice softened. "That is the truth."

"You said if I told the truth, you'd let me go."

"No. I promised we'd give you what you want. And this--" Ragvald's tongue flicked in time to Maddox's words. "--is what you want."

My hands fluttered on the pelts, grasping, clawing as if I could hang on to my control.

"You need to let me go--"

In answer, Maddox shifted his hand and drew my head to the side, baring the fragile line of neck and shoulder. He laid his mouth there, over my pulse, and sucked.

Ragvald moved closer to my center.

A moan started in me, echoing from a deep place inside where I locked every desire I shouldn't have.

"You are my captors. You keep me in this prison--"

"Wrong, little witch. We're the ones setting you free."

Something was building, building, my body mounting up like a bird winging towards the sun.

"And we'll never let you go."

Ragvald's mouth hit the right spot just as Maddox's teeth pierced the skin of my shoulder. The slight pain and the raging pleasure rolled together, and I convulsed, a leaf shaking in a storm. Shuddering, I was grateful for Maddox's powerful arms around me, his solid chest at my back. These arms could hurt me, and kill, but they could protect me.

Tears leaked out of the corner of my eyes. Ragvald came to lick them away. He pressed his mouth to mine, leaving my taste on my lips.

"Please." My defenses breached, I could ask for what I wanted, what I needed. "Please fill me."

My pleasure ebbed away, leaving a vast emptiness. I would do anything to have them take me. If they didn't, I would die.

"Patience." Ragnvald nuzzled my breasts. "You'll do as we command. If we desire you to take your pleasure a thousand times this night, you will obey."

"You will break me."

"Only your will. " His hands roamed over my body while Maddox pinned mine at my side. "The rest we will hold safe in our keeping."

"But--" I started to raise my voice, and Ragvald silenced me with a finger at my lips. "Hush now. This night, we are your masters. You serve our desires."

"Do not fear, Sabine," Maddox said. "We desire your pleasure. We will not let you deny your lust anymore."

"Or ours," Ragvald stroked my thigh. "If I could speak with the goddess, I would ask--how is it a mortal human can be so lovely?"

Maddox's hand traced the hollow at my hip. "She uses sugar gum to smooth her legs."

Folding my leg, Ragnvald kissed my knee, then licked it. His tongue blazed a trail higher and I felt my insides clench, ready for his wicked touch all over again. "I can taste the sweetness. Tart as well."

Maddox chuckled, a heady sound in my ear. I felt it rumble in his chest. "That is not sugar gum you are tasting, brother."

"It is divine." Ragnvald nuzzled between my legs for a moment. "The finest mead. Honey and spirits. It awakens a craving for more." He came to kiss me again, gently, refined. "We will never be satisfied with your sweetness, Sabine."

"Fortunately she has more to offer. Her sharp tongue."

"Mmm." Ragnvald drew out the kiss. "We know how to tame her."

They spent several minutes stroking my body, exploring every inch. If I struggled, one held me while the other continued. Maddox dipped his finger into my cunt. Ragnvald hefted my breasts. They touched me everywhere but where I needed it most, and my arousal danced up to a fever pitch.

"Please," I breathed. "I need you."

"Which one?" Ragnvald raised his head, the hunger in his eyes took my breath away.

"I-I cannot choose." If one of them left me, I could not bear it. Maddox shifted me in his arms so I could see his face as well as his warrior brother's. The moonlight shining into the cave was just enough to reveal all their naked need. "Both of you," I whispered finally, mouth dry. "I need both of you."

"We will give you what you need, sweet one." Ragnvald placed a hand on my leg. "How many men have you known? I ask so we will not hurt you when the time comes."

I could barely corral my thoughts.

Maddox reached down and pinched my nipple.

"How many, Sabine?"

"None. Only boys who wished they were men."

"Hmm." Ragnvald drew his loincloth aside and I drew in a ragged breath, both shocked and filled with wanting.

"You're bigger than any of the others," I choked out.

He did not smile, but I sensed his pleasure. A part of him was still man, and proud. "We will take you here," he touched the petals of my sex, not quite brushing the sensitive nub. "And here." His fingers slid to my bottom pucker, hovered over it. "But not tonight."

"No, please. I need you inside me."

"Like this?" Ragnvald dipped his fingers into my wet center, splaying the two of them to stretch me while his thumb ran along one plump lip and paused near my pleasure nub.

I whimpered as desire swelled in me, pressing against the inside of my mind. When he took his hand away, I cried out and kicked until Ragnvald weighted my legs down with his, keeping them apart.

"I love to hear her begging." Maddox shifted me in his arms, clamping one tighter around my waist just under my breasts.

Ragnvald's fingers returned to stroke me lightly. "Perhaps we should keep her like this until the next full moon. Aching, wet, chained to the bed." He blinked. "She likes this thought. She spasmed against my hand."

"We'll make you beg for all you need, food and water, and release," Maddox spun the tale.

"A fine game."

"Hold her, brother," Maddox offered me up to the Viking. "I have not gotten a taste yet."

They switched positions, moving me like a sack of grain between them. Not grain--a treasure made of ivory and pearl, with hair spun from gold--but as Ragnvald cradled me in his lap and Maddox drew my legs apart, I felt the dominance in their touch. I was their treasure, their possession. They would do what they wanted with me, for as long as they liked.

"Very nice," Maddox said. He sat between my legs, staring at my wet center. Ragnvald held me when I tried to wriggle away.

"Be still, Sabine."

I turned my face away from Maddox's intent look on my

cunt. "Please, just take me."

"Quiet," Maddox murmured. He touched me, one finger rimming my lower lips, but did nothing else. "Look at me."

I squeezed my eyes shut.

"Sabine. Do as I say."

The fist was back around my heart, squeezing, making me want to hide. These men had traveled and had many women. How could they look at me like I was the only one on earth they wanted?

"Sabine, I will not tell you again."

I obeyed.

"Keep your eyes on me," he ordered. As he continued with his feather-light exploration of my most intimate place, I fought the urge to close my eyes, fold my legs, and wriggle away.

Ragnvald flexed corded arms around me, holding me tighter, reminding me that he could easily control my struggles.

Maddox's hand fell on the center of my legs, slapping my cunt. I squealed and struggled, even as the slap made a wet sound.

"She likes it." Maddox licked the taste of me from his hand.

"Here," Ragnvald moved his legs to pin my quivering ones, moving them wider. "Do it again."

Another slap, then tender dancing fingers. Pleasure hit me like a fist, then danced just out of reach.

"Please. No more."

"Again," Ragnvald commanded, and with a wicked grin, Maddox complied. I howled, cursing them and writhing madly against Ragnvald's muscled frame. I wanted to fuck them, I wanted to kill them; desire made those acts one and the same.

"She likes it rough," Maddox observed. "Let's see how she likes this." Bending, he stroked his tongue up and down my slit with the lightest touch. I stopped struggling and melted into Ragnvald's hold. Maddox held my eyes. The sight of my pale legs framing his rawboned face was the most beautiful thing I'd ever seen.

A moan broke from deep within me, long and loud as a wolf's howl. Maddox never stopped driving me towards pleasure that would rival even that which Ragnvald had given me. My cunt throbbed like a wild thing. Eyes closed now, Maddox pressed his lips to my center in a worshipping kiss. His violence overpowered but his gentleness would undo me.

Maddox slid a finger into my bottom as he carried me to the precipice. I bucked when I realized how he'd invaded me, but between that and his mouth on my cunt, I was overcome. Pleasure took my mind, shaking me in its grip. It took me beyond the realm of words, stole my breath, turned my vision black.

When my eyesight returned, I saw Maddox before me, licking his lips.

"You satisfy Sabine."

"You more than satisfy," Ragnvald echoed. He slid away from me carefully, and laid me on the bed. Maddox went and wet a cloth, and returned to press it to my swollen, still throbbing flesh. Both men cleaned me and smoothed my hair, while I floated on the bed.

When they tucked the pelts around me and started to leave, I came awake.

"Wait, are you leaving? What about..." Their obvious arousal tented their clothes. "I can serve you. Please, I want to."

Crouched on the bed, I knew I looked like a siren,

blonde hair spilling down my back, nipples ruched and lips red from their kisses. I was willing, and aching. They hesitated, exchanging a glance.

"You are not ready, little witch."

"My body aches for you. Please fill me."

They looked torn.

They were not content with my desire. They had to own me.

"No, Sabine. You must be sure."

"When you give yourself to us, there will be no hesitation, no retreat. We will claim your body. Every part of you will be ours. You will belong to us for all time."

"And we will belong to you."

∽

As THE MOON climbed higher and disappeared beyond the cave roof, I lay on the bed, aching. The pleasure they'd given me had only whet my taste for more. But they refused to continue until they had my full surrender.

Raising my head, I met Maddox's eyes. Neither of the warriors slept. The scent of my arousal hung so thick in the air, even I could smell it. It would be torture for these men who became wolves.

Finally I rolled to my side to face them.

"Why?"

"We would do you a dishonor, to take you in your altered state."

I gripped the furs to keep from railing at them. I was supposed to be the strong one.

"When a wolf takes a mate, it is for life. They are bonded--connected with ties stronger than any pack or brother bond.

"I don't want to mate," I ground out. "I just want to fuck. Surely you can put aside your sense of honor for one night." My throat felt raw with frustration, and from screaming my pleasure earlier.

Maddox looked away. Ragnvald shook his head.

"I hate you," I snapped, and lay back down on the bed.

I could almost hear Maddox saying *That's good anger, little witch. Use it.*

If there was a way to seduce these warriors, without tying myself to them forever, I would find it. Rolling over, I curled on my side with a sigh.

It would be a long night.

∽

I SULKED through the morning even though I was alone until noon. Maddox finally emerged from the wood. The tight look on his face told me he was at the end of his control.

When I asked, he told me, "Ragnvald is with the pack. If you pray, little witch, ask for peace to rule that meeting. His beast will not respond well to threats."

'If his control is so fragile, why did you let him go?'

"He needs to establish his place in the pack. The meeting will reaffirm the pack bonds, deepen them, give the pack the strength they need to control their beast."

I huffed and went to and from the fire, heating water for cleaning..

Stripping the pelts to air them out.

I felt him at my back and stilled. "Do not worry, little witch. He will return soon."

"I do not care if he returns. I do not care to see either of you ever again."

"I know you think we're cruel."

"Of course I do. You stole me away in the night. Chained me to bait a monster. Imprisoned my sisters to ensure my cooperation." My cunt throbbed angrily, reminding me that none of these things mattered, I'd forgive Maddox, them and a world of sins if he'd just lay me down on the bed and fuck me. "And yet you won't touch me when I ask. Why do you not just let me go?"

Blowing out a breath, he started to march away.

"You care nothing for me," I muttered. As soon as he turned around, I knew I had made a mistake.

He walked past me without stopping, but snagged a fistful of hair to drag me back into the cave, beyond the clean, sandy floor where I made our home, into the dank, spiderwebbed recesses where darkness clawed at me. I gasped when things scuttled at my feet.

"Here," Maddox snarled, pointing to a large rock with the link where Ragnvald had been chained. The runes had kept him from breaking the iron and prying it off. "This is where I kept my best friend, a brother who saved my life countless times--every day, if you consider how he held my beast at bay. He accepted the taint on himself. And he never complained."

"You're hurting me." I cried.

"You are spoiled." He spat. "You have never known a day's worry--"

"I..?" I twisted and clawed at him until he let me go. "What would I give to be a man with one tenth your strength. I lived in fear, wolf. My mother married a man who beat her and raped my sister. He died before he could touch me, but not before he did away with my sister somehow. His death drove my mother to drink. I held the family together, and kept my sisters warm, sheltered, fed, all the while keeping the men of the village at bay. There has never been a day when I didn't wonder if I could go on walking the fine line between food or hunger, safety or disgrace. I survived." My fists curled at my sides. "I thrived. And then you took me and I will never be the same."

My voice echoed hollowly in the cave. My words, when they reached my ears, did not seem my own.

I wanted to go home. But home was gone. Even my sisters would be shaken from their illusion of safety. How could I protect them from what lurked in the large world?

"You've vowed to never join yourself to a man because you are trying to protect yourself. Did you wonder about how it is harming you?"

I scrubbed my hand over my face. "I need to go. Please, for just this afternoon, let me be."

"Come," he held out his hand. "I will take you to get herbs."

~

MADDOX CHOPPED wood while I kept my head down and gathered herbs along the banks of a woodland stream. Working side by side felt natural and benign, but my body still rang with my frustration and his harsh words.

The times I'd laid with a village man, I'd enjoy myself. There were the usual whispered promises and fervent pledges, but they hadn't meant anything beyond the heat of the moment.

My instincts told me these Berserkers would tie me to them, one way or another, and worse, I would forever long to be in their thrall.

Just watching Maddox wield his ax, tattoos snaking over mighty shoulders, cleaving a great oak with a force that sent wood chips flying, made me warm all over. If I dared think on last night, I would remember how my body felt like I'd waited my whole life for their touch.

They'd waited centuries for mine.

Turning my back to Maddox, I continued harvesting the succulents I needed. I was a healer, nothing more, nothing less. I could focus on my job, and find my place among these men before I lost myself.

After a few minutes I realized instead of the sound of an axe splitting a tree, there was only silence. Not the silence of a forest--full of insect noises and birdsong--but true silence, the sort that happens when a predator is about, and every prey animal holds its breath.

My hackles raised as I recognized a growling, snuffling sound in the brush. "Maddox?"

A shadow emerged from the trees, and I stumbled back before I remembered Maddox's wolf shape. This creature was bigger than any natural wolf, with thick black fur mottled with brown and a hint of sharp canines. It did not bare its teeth immediately and I gulped down my fear.

"Maddox, is that you?"

No answer from the great, dark wolf. I held my ground as it cocked its head at me, but when it growled again I couldn't keep myself from backing away. Tall enough to come almost to my shoulder, and half a length longer than me, the creature's most disturbing feature was its eyes, glowing with an otherwordly light.

Dropping my herbs I fled. A second later, the wolf's jaws snapped at my legs. I didn't have time to scream as I ran flat out towards the cave, praying that Maddox's beast would remember me.

I felt hot breath on my neck just as I swerved around a

tree and came face to face with Maddox tearing across the clearing to save me.

"Get down," he barked. I dropped and rolled, then hugged the ground as the wolf's defeated snarl blended with Maddox's angry roar. When I dared look, there was only a blur of black fur and tattooed muscle. Maddox had the wolf in his embrace.

I did scream then. Warrior though he was, Maddox would be no match for a great beast's fangs.

But when Maddox and the wolf broke apart, the warrior didn't look like a man any more. His body had grown, and his arms seemed longer, so as he hunched over they almost brushed the ground. Giant claws sprouted from his hands, and his canines flashed in his mouth.

My scream died in my throat.

"Sabine." Ragnvald was at my side, lifting and carrying me into the relative shelter of the cave.

I gripped his jerkin. "You must help him."

"He has the battle well in hand," Ragnvald assured, though he looked grim.

I risked a glance back but the fight must have moved into the forest, leaving a few broken trees in its wake.

"Were you hurt?" He set me down and ran his hands over me.

"I--" My head jerked towards a dark shape emerging from the forest. Maddox. The tattooed man looked tired, but human, even if his canines were unnaturally long.

I raced to him and Ragnvald let me go. Maddox caught me, holding me close but a little away from his body. His arms and chest were unmarked, but the breeches he'd been wearing were ragged and torn.

"What was that? Are you alright?" I started to search for wounds and Maddox gripped my wrists gently.

After a moment, he worked out a guttural growl, "I'm fine."

"You--you just ran at it...you didn't stop." I was gulping now, half way between a hiccup and a dry sob. I couldn't get enough air.

Maddox dropped my hands and pulled me into his arms.

"Relax now," his words rumbled under my ear as he cradled my head to his chest. "You're safe. No harm done."

"Breathe, Sabine." Ragnvald ordered. I focused on pulling air into my lungs.

"What happened?" Maddox spoke to his Alpha over my head.

"One of the pack. He must have followed me and smelled her. It's my fault--"

"No, it isn't," I pulled away from Maddox as far as his arms would let me. "I strayed too far--I was stupid--"

"Silence," Ragnvald commanded, not unkindly. "You are here by our will, and we have pledged you protection. We are Berserkers. There is no place in the entire world that you should fear to walk. Least of all our territory." He sighed and his kingly mien fell away. "That said, I'll ask you to stay close to one of us until I am stronger. When I am at my full power I'll be able to aid the weaker ones in their control. The blame lies with me, me alone." He inclined his head and waited for me to nod and accept his apology.

While Ragnvald loped off to deal with the intruder, Maddox remained. He seemed loath to let me go.

I fluttered my hands in the small space between us. "I'm alright. It just startled me, that's all."

"Look at me, little witch." A smile softened his features. My breath caught at the change. No longer just striking, his face looked handsome. "You seemed very worried about me."

"Of course," I rested my head back against him. "If you die, who will I hate?"

A chuckle vibrated under my cheek and I closed my eyes, finding peace in the perfect sound. Maddox just held me, and I let him stroke my hair back from my face.

The memory of his touch lingered when I finally drew away.

"There isn't a member of the pack who can best me. Even Ragnvald and I are equals. You have no need to fear."

I rolled my eyes. "I don't fear." When I tried to push away, he locked his arms around me.

"Do you have a kiss for your champion?"

"Let me go, Maddox. Or I'll tell Ragnvald I want to see who is the better fighter of you two. I'll stand back and pray that he rips out your tongue."

"Such sweet words, Sabine. If you really hated me, you'd ask him to cut my throat."

"Keep talking and I will."

∽

RAGNVALD RETURNED a short time later pretending to ignore Maddox while he grinned at me like a fool.

"It was Gunnr," the Alpha reported. "I called for his warrior brothers to keep watch over him."

"Is he all right?" I asked.

Ragnvald looked surprised that I'd ask after the well-being of my attacker.

I shrugged. "He is pack. If one of you is hurt, the rest feel it, yes?" I didn't know how I knew that, but Ragnvald's slow blink told me I was correct--and that I'd spoken a secret I shouldn't know.

At last, Ragnvald inclined his head. "Berserkers heal fast. Maddox just did enough damage to drive him off."

Maddox accepted the praise graciously. "No need to kill him. Gunnr scented Sabine and couldn't resist. I know the feeling."

"As do I. But this cannot stand," Ragnvald said in a harder tone. "His warrior brothers will keep him in wolf form, and they will run apart from the pack for a few days as punishment, and a warning to the rest of them. He will learn better control, or next time we will cut him from the pack."

I gulped. "Maddox told me that was certain death."

"A lone wolf is a dead wolf," Ragnvald agreed. "But it will be justice deserved for attacking what is mine. As the pack comes under my control, any who threaten you, or seek to claim what is not theirs to claim, will answer to me."

"And me," Maddox growled.

"Honor will return to the pack. The warriors will fall in line, under threat of banishment," Ragnvald said. "Until that day, we'll be careful to watch over you, little witch."

"I didn't run at first," I told him, ignoring the intense looks they both were giving me. "I thought it was Maddox."

'My wolf is darker. True black."

"It's not your fault, Sabine. I will lay down the rules. The stronger I am the more I can enforce them. As Alpha my control should be the best, and extend to the weaker members."

"If that is but one member of the pack, what of the others?" I had a horrible thought. "My sisters are with those men."

"Your sisters are safe." Ragnvald soothed. "We do not

keep them near the pack. Only the strongest members guard them."

"Besides, your sisters do not cycle with the moon as you do. When the heat is on you, your scent is a siren call," Maddox said.

I flushed.

Ragnvald cleared his throat. "Muriel and Fleur are not in any danger. I give you my word. Which reminds me," Ragnvald reached into his pouch, and handed me a floral crown made of vines braided together, one link of blue flowers and one with white. My twin sisters often made them for market. Muriel picked the vines, and Fleur did the weaving with her clever fingers.

"Thank you," I choked out. I brought the braid to my mouth and turned away, missing the twins so much I was dizzy. I felt relief that my sisters were safe, and amazement that fate would bring us to such a place, but no hate for my captors. Remembering the heat at my heels as the Berserker wolf attacked me, I searched for the hate, the censure, but it wasn't there. Not anymore.

That thought sent me reeling, and after I laid the braid down with my things, I covered my burning eyes.

"Sabine?"

My shoulders hunched even as gentle hands touched my hair.

"You need never hide from us, Sabine."

I gasped in pain as the knot in my chest unravelled, my tears coming unbidden as if all the fear I'd been carrying could be washed away. Strong arms lifted and carried me to the bed, where Ragnvald held and rocked me, Maddox stroked my arm while I cried.

"You're so strong. You don't need to be strong right now. Let us carry you a little while."

Covering my mouth so what I felt would not pour out, I untangled myself from their hold and sat on the bed. They hovered, stroking my back and hair.

"You take care of us," Ragnvald continued. "Can we take care of you? Can you trust us that far?"

"I can't. I made a vow, never to give in to a man." I stared hard at the ground. "I want you more than I thought possible. And I wish I didn't." My hands fluttered uselessly. "It tears me in two. I hate myself for it." I drew in a ragged breath, fighting for calm. "I wish I was made of stone."

"If you were you would not be who you are," Ragnvald murmured. "You would not be able to heal us."

I bit my lip. Love was weakness. If I gave in to it, I'd be tied to them forever. There would be no more Sabine without Maddox or Ragnvald. I couldn't risk it.

Maddox knelt before me. "Do you know how the Berserkers came to be?"

I blinked at the change of subject. "The witch turned them into warriors for the king."

"That's how it was for most of the pack, but not all. Not me." He held my hands and rested them in my lap as he told the story. "In my old country, Ériu, I was a prince set to be king. But I was proud. I believed my power came from ruling with a firm hand.

"One winter's night, an old woman came begging to my door, but instead of mercy, I sent her away. Three nights she came and asked for help. Three nights I spurned her request, thinking that indulging my serfs would make me look weak. The third night she shed her guise, and revealed herself to be a sorceress. Because I had not shown her mercy, she showed none to me. She cursed me with the tainted magic that left me a slavering beast. I became an outcast among my own people. If I could speak to my younger, proud self, I would tell him 'Kindness and mercy does not make a person weak.'"

"I can give you kindness and mercy, but..." A sob threatened to choke me.

"That's more than we deserve, after what we've done," Maddox murmured. Raising a cloth, he dabbed at my tears. "Maybe that will be enough."

I cupped his face in my hands, my fingers brushing the scars and blue whorls marking the decades. He'd lost everything. If he hadn't taken me, he'd have lost it again. There was no guile in his expression, just admiration, tenderness and something more.

"I'm sorry the witch cursed you."

"I'm not. It brought me to you." Turning his head, he kissed my palm. "And you are worth any pain."

I smiled, and his tongue turned teasing, nipping at my fingers.

Ragnvald swept the hair from my neck and nuzzled the shoulder opposite to the one Maddox had marked. I whimpered as their touches brought forth my desire, an ocean of arousal sweeping me under.

I spoke before I lost all good sense.

"How can you say such a thing? Surely it would've been better to never have met me than to face decades of struggle and pain."

"Perhaps," Maddox said. "But it was not to be." His hands dropped to my ankles, sliding up my legs, pushing up my gown. "I've accepted my destiny, little witch. It is time you accepted yours."

"Enough talking," Ragnvald spoke, but not to me. "We need to claim her. It is time."

Maddox came up on the bed and I pushed myself from Ragnvald's lap to sit between them.

"Claim me?" I turned my head to look at one, then the other.

"It will give you our protection. Keep you safe when you face the pack again."

"But what--"

"Shhh," Maddox set a finger against my lips. "You want this. I watched you dance around the affections of the men in the village. You were tired of them and took none to your bed. Would you have us return you to them, to break your heat? Do not lie," he added, with warning in his tone.

"No. I don't want them."

"Then you will stay," Ragnvald said. "Because we will not allow you to leave." He took one wrist and Maddox took the other, shackling me with rough hands and muscled arms as effectively as iron bonds.

My blood hummed and the scent of my arousal was thick enough to choke on. They'd taken away my choice, and I felt free.

"Now, brother, which of us should claim her first?" Ragnvald asked.

"I'll start, as I am the one who found and watched over her in the village, for moons and moons." Maddox pulled me to face him, and cupped my cheek. "And what a fine hunt it was." He kissed me and I kissed back, hungry, wanting. When he drew back he looked somber. "Today, in the woods, I could've lost you."

"No," I whispered. "You were there. I knew you'd protect me."

He groaned. "Sabine. I do not deserve the trust in your eyes."

Pushing the tattooed warrior to his back, I reared up over him and I did what I'd wanted to do since I first saw his naked form framed in the wilderness. Setting my mouth on

Maddox's chest, I used my tongue to trace the lines and whorls of his tattoos. His muscles danced under my mouth as his breathing grew harsh. I flicked my tongue against one nipple.

Maddox's breath caught. "You will be the death of me."

"A good way to die," Ragnvald said. He had his cock out and was slowly stroking its length as he watched us.

Kissing down the broad plate of Maddox's chest, I found the trail of dark hair leading between the hollow of his hips. He remained still as if the ridges and plains of his abdomen were really carved from stone, but when my tongue ventured lower, he tensed as if in pain.

I paused, raising my head.

His rough hands cradled my head. "Don't stop. Don't ever stop."

I turned my head and kissed his palm.

His hands were large, scarred, painted with bluish swirls under the coarse hair. They could lift a boulder, break iron bands, kill a man, but now they touched my temples and slid into my hair, drawing me back up over him and holding me still for his kiss.

He took my mouth as if he breathed a century of pain into me, and I let him, opening my mouth, inviting. When the kiss ended he kept one hand fisted in my hair and pressed our foreheads together.

"I've waited so long to touch you." The words rasped out like they'd been stored deep inside him, where they would never see the light of day. "When I first saw you I didn't think you were real." He brushed away a few strands that had fallen out of my braid. "Hair like honey, skin like milk. You were at your stall in the market, surrounded by wreaths of herbs and flowers. I wanted to buy you, and hold you in the palm of my hand."

I kept still, hovering over him as his hand skated down my bare form, between my breasts, over my belly, to cup me between the legs. Two of his fingers entered me. His touch rippled through my body, and in that moment, he owned me. He was a god and I was his priestess, a willing sacrifice, ready to throw myself on the pyre. His fingers moved inside me and I was no longer a woman, but a flame dancing to his desire.

With a grin, Maddox kept up the motion of his fingers until pleasure rippled through me. It made my insides prickle, an itch that could only be soothed by a hard cock inside me.

In one moment, Maddox lay licking his fingers clean, in the next, I was flat on my back, breathless, my arms pinned on either side of my head.

"Maddox." My hips started to move. "I want--"

"No, Sabine," Ragnvald said. "You do not make demands. You are ours and you do as we want."

I whimpered.

"Relax. Just be." Muscles taut, Maddox lowered himself until his cock brushed my entrance. I fought to push up and accept it into my body, but he kept me pinned while he held himself over me. Slowly, eyes on mine, he rolled his hips, teasing my folds with his iron cock.

Finally, I stopped struggling and relaxed under the warrior. My hands, captured in his, spread in supplication. "Please."

He kissed me, hard, and as his tongue breached my mouth, his cock thrust inside me. I accepted him deep into my body, a total claiming.

Rolling, he positioned me on top, where his cock filled me further still. Bouncing up and down, I turned into a wanton wild thing.

He popped out and I whined when he held me by the hips, refusing to set me back down on his cock.

"See to my warrior brother first."

My head bowed back as Ragnvald tugged on my hair, positioning me on all fours in front of Maddox. My cunt spasmed, howling silently with longing, and my body stayed lax and pliant for the Alpha as he moved me where he wanted me to go. The tight pain on my scalp made me gush, my body recognizing its master.

With a hand on the back of my neck, Ragnvald forced my head down and speared me from behind, beating into my haunches as I gripped the pelts. Maddox smiled as he watched Ragnvald take me, stroking his still hard cock. The sight sent pleasure pulsing through me.

Gripping my hair, Ragnvald pulled me up off the bed, to my knees. His teeth found my shoulder and bit down.

I cried out. Pain sparked a brushfire of pleasure and sent my orgasm roaring through me. The Alpha shouted as my rippling cunt milked him. For all his rough play, his hands, as he guided me back down to the bed, were gentle.

I blinked up at Maddox. I'd settled between his legs, my cheek almost on his thigh. His cock stood up like a standard. As soon as my body wasn't jelly, I crawled over and engulfed it with my mouth. Sucking until my cheeks hollowed and moans vibrated through me, I made him cum with a shout, then sat back, satisfied. Seed trickled from my lips and spilled from my folds.

Staring at the two men, I licked my lips slowly.

"Again?"

7

The moon shone down on us and lit the way to morning. We rose and crested together on the pelts, again and again, as the two warriors broke my heat and the goddess' spell upon me. My body moved between their bodies, one marked and the other pure, filled with the goddess' own power. Waves of desire crashed through me, beating at my core, washing away all my walls and battlements. The roar of my orgasm overwhelmed me, bowed me back, but my lovers held me, kept my body safe while my thoughts seared through the sky like a shooting star.

When I came down, they cradled and rocked me.

～

UPON WAKING MIDMORNING, Ragnvald gave me a swift kiss and left to meet with the pack. Maddox stayed, whistling as he stacked wood near our fire. I waited until his back was turned, then crouched down with a wet cloth to wipe down my legs and the tender folds between my legs. I had a few bruises, I noted with satisfaction, and my sex was sore and puffy. The cool water felt good.

A shadow fell over me, and I hastily rose and tossed the cloth away. "What's this, Sabine? Still shy around your lovers?"

"I am not your lover, wolf," I straightened my gown.

His astonished pause almost made me laugh. "What of last night?"

"That was lust," I told him haughtily.

The shock fled, leaving a wicked smirk. I backed away as he stalked me.

"Was it lust when you tackled me when I tried to leave the bed? Lust when you screamed my name and made me promise to remain inside you forever? You marked me." He turned and showed me raw scratches on his back.

"I'm sorry--"

"I'm not." He stilled. "Do you regret what we did, Sabine?"

"No, no," I said impatiently. "I enjoyed it. I allowed it."

Maddox crowded closer, frowning. "That's not what I asked."

I snatched up a pelt and clutched it to my front. "While the sun is high I'm going to air these."

Maddox tugged the fur before I could rush away. "Sabine. Tell me what's wrong."

"Nothing's wrong. You're just making last night into something more than it is." I called up my annoyance. "Now leave me be."

He let me go, but a harsh order made me halt. "Remember the rules, Sabine. No lying."

"I am not lying. Last night, I wanted you, you wanted me, and we enjoyed ourselves."

"And?"

"And...nothing .What is there left to say? You took my body--" I blushed, "many times. I am grateful. The heat settles after the full moon, but when I abstain, the desire never fully goes away."

"And now? Is the desire gone?"

I paused. The moon lust was gone, but now a warmer, softer feeling pulsed through me. "The estrous has ended. I am replete."

His voice dropped to a deep rumble I felt in the cradle of my hips. "Do you remember at the beginning? We vowed we would claim you."

"I remember. As I said, you took nothing I wasn't willing to give."

"That's not how claiming works."

"How does it work then, wolf?"

A broad grin. "I would tell you. But it will be more fun to show you."

I all but threw my hands up in the air. "Fine."

Maddox went on chuckling. "I'll tell Ragnvald you don't believe you belong to us when he returns."

"I don't belong to you."

His grin only got wider. "Oh yes," he said. "This is going to be fun."

∼

But when Ragnvald returned, they spoke only of the well being of the pack. I listened with interest.

"Gunnr's warrior brothers took him on a long scouting mission. They'll watch the border. The beast will be happy to take out its frustration on any unwelcome intruders, and if it does break free, they'll be far from any temptation."

"What is a warrior brother?" I asked.

"Warriors in the pack who share a closer bond. We're all tied together, as you guessed, but some closer than others. As Alpha, I can sense anyone in the pack, pull strength from the many to aid the few."

"How does the brother bond form?"

"Pack magic does what it will," Ragnvald shrugged.

"I know how ours formed," Maddox said. "I saved Ragnvald's life, and he saved mine. The bond between us grew stronger after that."

"Did the beast weaken it?"

"Only because I let it," Ragnvald said. "If I slipped into madness, I didn't want to drag Maddox down with me. So I let the beast gnaw and fray it."

"I would that you hadn't," Maddox said quietly. "I might have helped you for longer, if our bond had remained strong." Silence stretched between them, full of untold pain.

"Can it be repaired?" I kept my voice brisk.

"It can," Maddox answered in a happier tone. "It already has been. The bond allows two dominant wolves to work together, rather than fighting. It's how we can lead the pack as equals, and share a woman."

"Not just share her. Mate with her," Ragnvald said. Before he could say more, I interrupted.

"Looks like rain is coming. Can you take me to the stream before it falls? I'd like to gather more soapwort before a frost."

Amused, the Alpha agreed. I ignored Maddox's chuckling.

∽

That afternoon, a heavy rain kept us inside. I busied myself organizing my herbs, while Maddox honed a blade and Ragnvald stared at the fire, the intensity of his gaze telling me he was deep in his head. Probably repairing the pack bond even though he looked like he was doing nothing at all.

The memory of our lovemaking lingered. The men had their own way of not letting me forget it--a brush of a hand, a gentle tug of my hair as I moved past them to the fire, a million little touches that sent my body humming. They'd bound me again, this time without a chain. They'd shackled my thoughts to them, and even if they let me go, I would never be the same again.

I started pacing at the mouth of the cave, staring at the restless forest beyond the waves of rain.

"Restless, Sabine?" Maddox called to me. "We can find something for you to do." When I whirled, hands on hips, he added, "Unless last night wrung all the lust out of your delicious body. No," he raised a finger. "Don't lie. We can smell you from here."

"Fine. I want you. Both of you." I raised my chin. "It doesn't have to mean anything."

"Someday we will punish you for lying--not just to us, but to yourself. Until then, you suffer enough, denying what you want."

"And what do I want?" As soon as I spoke it, I knew how dangerous the question was.

Maddox set down his work and came to me. "Everything. You want everything."

"And we pledge the same to you." Ragnvald hadn't lost his look of fierce concentration but he no longer directed it towards the fire. "Everything we have to give is yours."

I made a show of glancing around the cave. "As much as I...enjoy your company, once you are healed, I'd prefer to return to the village."

"And what waits for you there?" Maddox asked. "A life of drudgery? Marry a brute, bear him fifteen squalling babes, hoping a handful live?"

I pressed my lips together.

"Sabine. You can be more. We can be more."

I shook my head. "I can't...please."

"Maddox," Ragnvald sounded tired. "Let her alone."

"Very well. I will leave it...for now. There are more interesting things to attend to." His smile turned playful. "For one, there is the matter of your punishment."

"Punishment? Beyond this exile?" I waved my hand about, even though the cave had become an almost pleasant place. "What else will you do to me? Chain me up outside in the rain?"

"Of course not," Maddox scoffed. "Who would warm our cocks tonight?"

I threw a pelt at his head, and he caught it.

"Certainly not me."

He tapped his nose. "Another lie. Just the mention of punishment is enough to get you excited. I wonder why that is?"

Crossing my arms in front of me, I decided to play along. Need pulsed through my core, not the heat of the moon, but a different, earthier feeling, as if last night had only opened the door to desire, and given me a taste of what I could have. A raindrop, and now I wanted an ocean.

"Very well. I'm curious. What are you disciplining me for?"

"Earlier, you denied belonging to us. You are ours, Sabine, and it's time you learned what that means."

He backed away and nodded to Ragnvald. Their mood was light, jovial, as if they were playing a well scripted game. Neither smiled, though.

"You are under our care. If you misbehave, there will be consequences."

"Consequences?"

"The pack relies on a careful balance of power," Ragnvald said. "Those who challenge someone stronger get put in their place. But females are rare. They are often weaker and must be treasured. Human mates are the weakest of all. So werewolves discipline their mates differently."

"You'll beat me, then?"

"Not exactly."

"What then?"

Maddox pounced. I found myself face down over his lap with my gunna around my waist. I kicked wildly. "What are you doing?"

"Showing you how you will be punished." He smoothed a hand over my bottom and squeezed each cheek.

"Stop it!"

My struggles only resulted in him pinning my legs under one of his and securing my hands in the small of my back. My feet fluttered as he caressed my bottom and then brought his hand down, hard.

My outrage echoed through the cavern. I tried twisting and Maddox held me further.

"That's one," he said, and smacked me again, harder. This time it stung.

"That's enough!"

"No, that's two."

Ragnvald laughed. I cursed at him, and gasped when Maddox let fly a flurry of smacks that had me dancing on my belly. The sting wasn't unbearable, but the humiliation of being pinned and punished like a naughty child was.

"I will kill you, wolf."

Maddox responded by slapping the tops of my thighs.

The pain on my sensitive flesh brought tears to my eyes, and I found it wise to say silent.

"Think she's learned her lesson?"

"I will ask her," Maddox said. "Will you obey us, Sabine? You may not speak, only nod."

"I--"

A fresh volley on my bare bottom had me gritting my teeth,.

"Let's try that again. Will you obey? You do not have permission to speak."

I jerked my head, once.

"Good girl."

He didn't stop spanking me, but varied the blows. They came hard and fast, sharp and slow, on all quadrants of my rounded bottom. My least favorite were the smacks to the tender tops of my thighs. I no longer fought, but try as I might I couldn't anticipate the blows.

I tensed as Maddox chopped his hand down repeatedly on one spot until it was warm, and then the other.

"Breathe, Sabine," he ordered, and I realized I'd been holding my breath and let it out in a rush.

Let go, something inside me whispered.

I relaxed under the onslaught, and immediately a sense of peace filled my body. These were my men and they would not hurt me.

Maddox must have sensed my surrender, for he stopped and squeezed my bottom cheeks, pushing the sense of euphoria higher.

"You're doing so well. And your bottom is a nice, pleasing pink." He added two sharp volleys on my sit spots. Pain rushed into my head, and morphed, turning into something more. My cunt ached, open, needy.

I cried out, pushing into his hand as it curved on my bottom.

He cupped it, enjoying the heat, but his fingers dipped between my legs and I moaned again. My back arched, seeking his touch.

"By the moon," he breathed. "You're soaked."

Ragnvald laughed.

As soon as he let go, I twisted in his arms, hands like claws to attack him. He caught me easily, and stared at me in surprise as I snapped my teeth and growled in his face. My struggles grew and his hands tightened on my wrists.

"Stop it," he ordered, and when that didn't calm me, he flipped me to my back and pinned me that way.

My hips rose up, begging. I whined and panted, a wanton, wild creature made of desire.

"Looks like you unleashed the wolf in her," Ragnvald chuckled. "I can smell her musk from here."

Holding me down under him, Maddox stared at me. I bared my teeth but didn't speak. I didn't need to speak.

"What are you going to do with her?" I heard Ragnvald moving closer.

"Fuck her," Maddox's deep voice made me clench with need. "Fuck her hard." His body dropped onto mine, pressing against the right spots with delicious intent.

"Is this what you want?" His hips swiveled, and his cock ground against my center. "You may speak."

"Yes," I whined. "Please."

"You were bad, attacking me. What do you call a little one who bites her master?"

"Bad. I'm very bad." I'd admit anything if he'd keep the movement of his hips against mine. "Please..."

"What do you deserve?"

"Punishment."

"You enjoyed the last one too much. It didn't teach you at all."

"Perhaps a different punishment then," Ragnvald suggested.

Maddox flipped me over. "All fours, Sabine. Push your bottom up into the air."

I waited like that until something cool spread in the crevice of my bottom. I leaped forward. "What's that?"

"No," Maddox's hand cracked on my bare cheek. "Hands and knees. You will obey."

Reluctantly I knelt again. Maddox pulled my gown over my head while Ragnvald busied himself behind me.

"Deep breath, Sabine. In and out." Something pushed against my back pucker, burning and then popping in. "This will stretch you for us, so that one day we might claim you together."

I moaned at the strange sensation, but my cunt dripped in readiness. "Please fuck me."

"Please me first," Maddox presented his cock to my lips. I sucked him down, working as hard as I could. The place between my legs felt so empty.

Ragnvald twisted the bulb in my backside, pushing and pulling, stretching me until I felt a flicker of sensation there.

"Focus," Maddox caught my head. "Give me pleasure."

"I'm going to spank you now." Ragnvald said. "Bite him, and we'll hang you by your wrists from a tree outside and whip you up and down until every part of you is striped. Understand?"

I nodded. With a hand in my hair, he guided me to swallow Maddox down. As I sucked, Ragnvald's hard palm caught the underside of my bottom, pushing me forward. The swats stung, but were bearable. I bobbed my head obediently as Ragnvald punished me. My pussy throbbed and I couldn't take it anymore.

"Please, please," I gurgled around Maddox's cock.

Ragnvald knelt behind me and grabbed my hair, drawing it back. "The plug stays in." He sank into my wetness, blissfully deep.

The warriors moved together, one at my back and one at my mouth. The plug made me feel full to bursting.

Moans shook me, shuddering, using my tongue on Maddox' cock.

"Subdue her."

Ragnvald's fingers bit into my hips. He cursed as he came deep inside me. I quivered barely staying on all fours.

Maddox steadied me with a hand, a gentle hand.

"Switch."

The second I tasted myself on Ragnvald, I was lost. I went wild lapping at my own taste as if I couldn't get enough.

"By the gods," he breathed.

"Get ready," Maddox warned.

"Open up," Ragnvald had me take his still-hard cock into my mouth.

Maddox braced my hips and then began to pound into me.

On the second stroke, I came. Frantic, I gurgled around Ragnvald's cock and he pulled out. Gasping, I dropped my head and hung on for dear life.

"This is how we fuck naughty ones who forget their place. On your hands and knees, helpless."

I rocked forward with each thrust. My fists gripped the pelts but did little to stop me from plowing forward. One orgasm gone and past, I sped towards the next, my cunt sucking Maddox in greedily, my bottom rising back, arching to take more in.

Ragnvald's cock danced in front of me, smacking my cheeks before he gripped it and stroked it.

Maddox grunted and bathed my bottom with his cum.

"You're lucky. Next time we punish you, we'll fuck you and leave our seed drying on your skin. You will get no pleasure, just scent of our release." He smacked my bottom in warning, but I only purred in satisfaction.

~

THAT NIGHT, the men never stopped touching me, and barely let me stand on my own. While Maddox roasted meat, Ragnvald held me on his lap and gave me sips from the horn he held. The drink tasted rich and heady, and I soon grew giddy. When the food was done, Maddox fed me choice scraps and made me lick his fingers. I wrapped my tongue around each digit, giggling at the game.

As the moon grew high, I lay on a pelt between them. Maddox rubbed my feet and Ragnvald stroked my hair as they sat and told stories of their past. The wind blew up some sparks and I lifted my hand as if I could catch them.

Ragnvald smiled down at me. "So Sabine, how do you like being a Berserkers' consort?"

The men's touch already sent flames licking between my legs. My voice came breathy and eager. "I am content."

Maddox chuckled. "We've found the way to satisfy our woman. Spank then fuck her." He raised my foot and kissed my toes to ease the arrogance in his tone.

"Am I your woman then?" I was too relaxed to argue.

"You have been, for sometime, or you wouldn't have been able to heal Ragnvald."

I supposed it was true. "How did you know I was the one? That the witch wasn't lying to you?"

Ragnvald and Maddox exchanged glances in one of their long pauses. "Your sister."

"Which sister? Muriel or Fleur."

"Neither." He paused long enough for me to guess what he would say, and for my heart to plummet to my feet in response. "Brenna."

I sat up. "You know her? Where is she-- can you take me to her--"

"She belongs to another Berserker pack," Ragnvald said. "Your stepfather sold her to them. They'd searched a long time, as we had for the woman a witch foretold--one marked by a wolf."

"Marked by the wolf?" I asked, and realized in the next instant. "Her scar from the dog attack."

"Yes. She was attacked by a wolf when she was young. The magic was strong in her and we believe drew a rabid werewolf to her. It tried to mate with her."

"Mate with her?"

"Bite her," he gestured to his shoulder. I realized both warriors had nipped at my shoulders during our love making. "Mating bites. She wears them now, from her true mates, the alphas that claimed her."

My hand rested at my throat where a knot had formed. Somehow I choked out what I had believed in my heart, but never thought I'd know for sure. "She's alive."

"And well," Maddox said. "She wishes to see you, too."

"We didn't tell you of her right away because in the past her pack and ours have quarrelled, and we knew little beyond that she lived. We've sent emissaries back and forth, for you and your sister's sake."

"When will I see her?"

"There is an assembly--a Gathering, much like the ones we had Her mates will be there. We will bring you and present you, make peace with them, and then you will be able to see your sister."

My hand slid to my chest, where the joyful pain made it hard to breathe. Maddox slid to his knees in front of me and took my hand.

"I thought you'd taken everything away from me," I whispered. "But...now it seems you are the ones returning it."

"We feel the same, little one," Ragnvald murmured at my back.

"We are your destiny," Maddox said, and for once I did not fight his claim.

"Before we meet Brenna's pack at the Gathering, you must meet ours." Ragnvald told me. "They want to thank the woman who saved them."

I agreed, and when the day dawned, I requested we go first to the stream so I could bathe and ready myself.

As I came up out of the water, wringing out my hair, I wished I had a new overdress, instead of the old tired one I'd rinsed and laid out on the bush to dry. After shrugging on my shift, I went to fetch the gunna, but it was gone.

"Looking for this?" Maddox stepped from the trees holding a gown--not my old overdress, but a new one--a lovely brocade in gold and green.

"Where did you get it?"

I noted he looked very handsome with new deerskin breeches and slicked back hair from his own dip in the pool.

"We sent a wolf to market. Can't have you naked when you meet the pack--much as they'd enjoy it." Maddox laid the dress down. "But first..." Lifting me, he sat on the nearest log, undid his breeches and set me on his cock. I grabbed his shoulders, arching back as he filled me. Hands on my waist, he bounced me on his thick rod until my cries echoed off the waterfall.

"What was that for?" I sagged forward after my orgasm.

"Marking you," Ragnvald spoke from behind me.

Maddox pulled me off with a plop, and steadied me as Ragnvald bent me forward and fucked me from behind. The blond warrior pulled out at the last minute, splashing his seed on the back of my legs.

"I just bathed!" I protested.

"Aye," Maddox said with a grin. "And now you smell like us again. And we smell like you."

When I turned, Ragnvald had the gown ready, and he helped me into my clothes. Both men wore new breeches and boots, though their chests were bare.

"One more gift." Maddox tied back my hair, and Ragnvald produced a silver torc, twisted with gold filaments, that matched the arm rings they wore around their powerful biceps.

"This torc claims you as ours," Ragnvald said, and bent it around my neck with an air of ceremony. "I pledge myself to you, Sabine of Alba. I will live and die for you, and keep you in my highest care," he said with a light kiss, and Maddox repeated the action and the words.

"Come," Maddox held his hand out to me. I took it, feeling joy and dread at the same time. So much had changed. I thought these warriors had ripped my life apart, but now they seemed to be working to bring my family together.

"You understand we will do what we must to protect you?" Maddox asked.

"Yes."

Maddox nodded to Ragnvald, who continued, "There

are rules you must obey, Sabine. This meeting with the pack will test you, and ready you for joining us at the Gathering. You must never disobey us in public. Keep silent, and keep your head bowed and eyes on the ground."

I sucked in a breath. "What?"

Ragnvald spoke in a slow, serious voice. "Those are the terms. Wolves expect a level of submission from their women."

"I am not a wolf."

"No, but you belong to us. You are one with us, and through us you are part of the pack. You will abide by pack law, or be punished."

I gritted my teeth. Ragnvald waited for a sharp retort that never came.

At last he nodded. "This is the final rule: you will stay behind me at all times."

"How will I know where to go, if my eyes are on the ground?"

Lifting a small, light chain, he attached it to the torc. "You'll follow my lead."

"No," I said, but he stepped away and tugged the metal tether.

I forced myself not to rail at him. "You will lead me like a dog?"

"You're lucky it's not on your hands and knees, like a female wolf." Again he pulled on the lead. I grabbed it to keep from moving forward.

"I--" My words died in my throat. I wanted to see my sisters but I didn't want to do this. "This is humiliating."

"Wolves and warriors live and die by strict laws. Unwritten, but laws just the same. We all have to find our place in the pack. I am the leader. Even though he was an outsider at first, Maddox is stronger and smarter than the others, and he saved my life. The pack accepts him as my second."

"I had to fight for it. Still do, at times," Maddox added.

"But you cannot fight. Even if we did allow you to challenge for dominance, you could not defeat the weakest warrior, Sabine. That puts you at the bottom of the pack. This chain protects you, claims you as ours."

"It makes me feel like a slave." My cheeks burned, with anger and embarrassment, and something more. Chained and collared, with the end of the leash in Ragnvald hand, I felt like a war prize, fought over and desired. My treacherous body responded to this as it had the rough fucking five minutes ago. The grin on Maddox's face told me the warriors could scent my true feelings.

"Slave or consort, what's the difference?" Maddox said. "You come and go by our leave. You eat what we give you. You share our bed."

I glared at him. "I will not be doing that anymore."

He laughed. "Very well. We won't force you." He brushed the back of his hand against my cheek before stepping away. "We'll let you beg for it."

"You are ours," Ragnvald said, and I couldn't deny the desire that built in me at his firm claim. "Ours to treasure. Ours to possess. And you will obey."

"I don't want to do this," I whispered.

With a sigh, Ragnvald wrapped the links around his hand, shortening the lead and drawing me closer. But when he spoke his voice was gentle. "This chain protects you. We will not visit the pack without you wearing it. One day you will be able to go without it. When the beast is trained, and we live as men and women do. But for now...it is too dangerous. We keep the pack rules. For everyone's safety."

My stomach roiled at the thought of being presented to

the pack like chattel. But I would do it, if not for my warriors, then for Muriel and Fleur. I took a deep breath. "I'll wear it. Just, please, when we see my sisters..."

"We will not make you wear it in front of them. We keep them separate from the pack, and will remove it when it is only us and the women."

"But you will wear the torc. Always," Maddox insisted.

I fingered the delicate links. "Very well."

With a small smile of approval, Ragnvald walked forward. I let him lead me, almost brushing his side with my eyes on the ground. It was easier to keep my gaze downcast while following his lead.

"That's it, Sabine. Stay close to me," Ragnvald sounded very pleased, almost proud.

We trekked through the forest, and I forgot my shame. The day was so nice, I lifted my eyes to the birds flying, the golden light filtering through the canopy. The further we trekked, the more I smelled a heady scent, wild and unfamiliar. I heard a roaring in the distance and finally asked what it was.

"The sea," Maddox said. He kept a close guard on our rear as we broke from the trees. Ragnvald stopped and I almost forgot myself and moved beyond him. The tight leash brought me up short. Cheeks burning again, I took my place at Ragnvald's side, a step behind. The tall leader looked very serious.

"Remember, Sabine, do not look any of the pack in the eyes. That is a challenge to a wolf, and will not end well for you, or any wolf that dared follow through."

I clenched my jaw.

"If you can't look down, look at Ragnvald or me," Maddox whispered. "Anywhere else, and you will be punished." His tone of voice was serious, but a twinkle in his eye told me he'd enjoy punishing me.

Lip curled, I bared my teeth at him like a wolf. He laughed.

"Keep that courage, little witch."

"Come," Ragnvald said, and his sober tone settled us. We walked through a field, navigating around great boulders. The grass was scrub turf and when I risked a peek at the horizon I saw only sky beyond a green rise, as if the land fell away.

"The cliffs overlook the sea," Maddox said. "Men rarely come here so we made it our home. The sight and sound of the ocean can be soothing."

"I've never seen it," I whispered back.

"Someday I will take you sailing." Maddox smiled at me. It made his face so charming, my heart thumped even though I was nervous.

"You've been on a boat?" I said, before I remembered his story.

"Of course. How do you think I got here? Quiet now." Two men stepped out from behind one of the boulders, looking as ragged as Maddox and Ragnvald had when we first met. I quickly dropped my eyes. I hated playing the part of a submissive captive, but when Maddox caught my hand and squeezed it, I felt better.

Ragnvald spoke to the men in a low, guttural language before switching to a language I knew. I stayed alert waiting for him to lead me forward. When he did I kept my gaze down but watched from the corner of my eyes.

The pack had made camp in the center of a circle of large boulders. Men ranged around a large fire pit. They greeted Ragnvald with a fist on their chest and downcast eyes. Acknowledging each with a nod, the blond leader went forward to one central boulder and stepped up to a ledge to look out over the assembled warriors. Even with my gaze fixed on the ground, I felt the weight of their gaze.

"Kneel, Sabine," Maddox murmured, and tossed a pelt on the ground for me.

Ragnvald sat and Maddox stood hovering at my right.

Under the scrutiny of all the warriors, I clutched Ragnvald's leg. Images ran through my head--I could not look at the men, but in my mind's eye I saw them--fighting, hunting, destroying. They went into battle wearing only wolf pelts and loincloths, and the enemy's axes and blades barely marked their skin.

Maddox dipped his head to whisper in my ear. His voice grounded me, but it took a moment to understand what he was saying. "They can't take their eyes off you. You are the most beautiful creature they've ever seen."

The pace of my heart eased as Ragnvald addressed the assembled pack.

"Berserkers, I gathered you here to meet Sabine, the healer who saved me. Though she is the weakest in our pack, she holds a place of highest honor, and the debt we owe her can never be repaid. Because of her healing arts, when we meet with the mountain Berserker pack in a few days, we will be strong enough to face them as equals."

At this, the warriors cheered, rattling their weapons and beating their shields in a terrifying din.

"Sabine, rise," Ragnvald commanded, and Maddox helped me up when I did not move quickly enough. The warriors cheered louder as the two Alphas flanked me, one at either arm. Humbled and yet exalted, I no longer felt like a slave or a piece of meat, but an esteemed guest.

"Take Sabine to her sisters while I speak to the pack," Ragnvald handed my leash to Maddox. I kept my eyes down but chin up as I passed the still shouting men.

"A good thing the pack accepts you, Sabine. You do not look docile in the least."

I schooled my features to be blank. He suppressed a laugh. "No matter. Humility doesn't become you."

We were out of earshot, close to the trees.

"You will be lucky if I share your bed ever again, wolf," I threatened.

He jerked the lead and I resisted before taking a step forward. He drew me inexorably closer, and I resisted as much as I could without it looking like I was disobeying..

"Impossible. I smell your heat from here. They all can." His eyes were bright. "They long for you. As soon as our business is done, Ragnvald and I will take you back to the cave and take you over and over until you scream our names." A tremor ran through me, weakening my legs, and Maddox slipped an arm around my waist and escorted me to the forest.

As soon as we were out of sight of the pack, the tattooed warrior dropped my leash. I surged onto my tiptoes, burying my hand in his hair as he claimed my mouth with savage longing. Wrapping a leg around his waist, I ground myself against him and he hefted me up in his arms, rubbing me until I shuddered with tiny shocks of pleasure. When he finally let me down, I sagged against him, panting. Maddox kept his hand in my hair, gripping it hard, tugging and releasing. I relaxed into his claim.

"Some packs pass their women around, and claim them during their heat at the main campfire for all the men to watch. Would that excite you or make you afraid?"

I whimpered, rocking against him.

"But we will never let you be claimed by another,

Sabine," he whispered fiercely. "I would go to the grave before I see another touch you."

Someone cleared his throat behind us and Maddox and I sprang apart.

Ragnvald raised a brow at us, but came to unhook the chain.

"You did well," Ragnvald said, pocketing the chain. I had a perverse vision of him leading me back to the cave where he and Maddox kept me crawling for the day, begging for their cocks. When I sighed, Ragnvald smiled as if he knew my thoughts.

"Your sisters are a short walk away," he said to calm me.

Nodding, I ran shaky fingers through my hair to smooth it.

Ragnvald held out his hand; I took it while Maddox claimed my other, and we walked on together. The trail led to a clearing beside a lovely little brook. A large, fine tent, tall and grand as a king's, stood in the center of the small meadow. A bearskin rug lay on the ground at the entrance. As we approached, a beautiful brunette poked her head out.

"Sabine," she said with a smile.

I stood transfixed. The woman looked so like Brenna, but shorter.

The smile faltered. "Sister, it's me. Muriel."

"Hello Sabine," a weaker voice spoke, and Fleur followed her twin to greet me. She seemed taller and more willowy than I'd see her before.

"I know," I let out a shaky laugh. "I...you look so grown up."

"Only by a sennight. It has not been so long," Muriel laughed and we rushed to hug each other.

Ragnvald and Maddox held back.

"Those are the pack Alphas," I whispered to my sisters, but they did not seem afraid.

"We know. Maddox is the one who came to explain where you were, and why the Berserkers took us." Muriel gave them a little wave. I noted that she kept her eyes lowered. Maddox must've warned her of the pack laws.

"We were frightened at first, but then grateful that they moved us," Fleur added.

"Moved us?"

"Yes. They heard Father Brexton was going to rally the villagers against you. It wasn't safe so they came for us."

I gave Maddox a sharp glance but he only shrugged. He'd probably told the tale to keep my sisters from panicking, and I should feel grateful, but I did not.

Muriel smiled right at Ragnvald. "Glad you're doing better, sir."

"As am I, Muriel," he acknowledged her with a graceful nod, and then turned to her twin. "Fleur, are you feeling better?"

"Has she been ill?" I asked Muriel, for we often nursed our youngest sibling through fevers and ague.

"The usual, but only for a little while," Fleur spoke up. "You don't need to talk about me like I'm a child. I can speak for myself."

I opened my mouth and closed it.

"And anyway, I'm better now. We got the herbs we needed. We even helped one of the pack find some wild honey."

"I thought you kept them away from the pack." I spoke to Ragnvald and Maddox, keeping my eyes lowered, and tone one iota away from disrespect.

"For their safety we post regular guards, and several of the men have befriended them." He held up a hand before I could issue a retort. "Your sisters are treated with the utmost respect."

"Come, " Muriel said soothingly. "See our living quarters." She held open the flap for me.

"We will build up the fire," Ragnvald said. "The pack is bringing meat for your dinner."

"Come on, Sabine," Muriel pulled me inside before I could protest.

The inside of the tent was richly appointed, with bearskin rugs lining the floor, and a few carved wooden chairs and braziers.

"So they treat you well?" I asked, still unhappy. I hated the thought of my sisters kept in the woods with only Berserkers for company.

"Of course," Muriel said.

"The first few nights were hard..." Fleur started, and Muriel cleared her throat. "But since then we've been treated well."

"Very well," Muriel flushed a little, and I frowned.

"Do you understand who these men are?"

"Werewolves." Muriel nodded. "And some aren't in control of their beast. They've gotten better, though. You've helped them with that?"

"Yes."

"They say the power runs in our family," Fleur said from her seat.

"Can you tell us more about that?" Muriel asked.

"I--" I hesitated, not sure how much I could say.

"We know you're a healer," Muriel went on when I would not. "And we all have something that calls to these wolves. An affinity." Her amused smile told me she'd seen me and the Alphas holding hands.

"What we want to know is how they found us."

Facing these two, who seemed so much older than I last remembered, lifted a weight from my shoulders. I dropped into a carven chair as if my legs had given out. "Brenna is alive."

Both my sisters went still, but not with shock. With expectation. In that moment I realized we'd all known Brenna's disappearance didn't mean her death. I hadn't spoken to Muriel and Fleur of it because I thought them children. If they were strong enough to survive capture and imprisonment, they'd earned the right to know of the magic in their blood.

"A Berserker tribe--not Ragnvald's, another one--went to a witch and heard the prophecy of a woman who could tame the beast. They found Brenna by looking for a woman with a scar."

Muriel nodded.

"Our stepfather sold her to them. Ragnvald and Maddox heard of her, and remembered a similar prophecy spoken to them. Maddox found me in the grove..." Here I blushed.

"And took you to heal them," Muriel finished smoothly, and I inclined my head, grateful.

"What now?" Fleur asked.

"I have bargained for our freedom."

"What about Brenna? Can we see her?"

"There is a meeting in a few days time. My Alphas--the Alphas of this pack--have promised that I may see her. I hold out in hope they will keep their word."

"We will, Sabine," Ragnvald said from the entryway. "We are in negotiations with Brenna's pack to guarantee safe passage for both you and your elder sister. You two are of utmost importance to our packs." He stooped to enter the tent. I clenched my hands in my lap at the rush of warmth I felt just at the sight of him. I had to remember he and

Maddox were our captors, and one day I would free myself and my sisters from them.

Unless you don't want to be free. Ignoring that traitorous part of me, I said, "Thank you, my lord. We are grateful for your care."

With a slight smile that told me he knew why I clung to formality around my sisters, he addressed Muriel and Fleur. "Perhaps if this first meeting goes well, we will host Brenna here for a visit. Or escort you to her."

My sisters thanked him politely as if he'd granted a boon, rather than decreed who might visit and when they could leave. Maddox called to us then, and we all adjourned outside to eat the venison he'd cooked over an open flame.

We sat and talked of mundane things--the weather, the herbs that grew by the stream. As the sun sank, I noted how Ragnvald looked more tired, the shadows under his eyes deepening. Maddox caught my eye and gave me a subtle nod before he began cleaning up around the fire.

"Walk with me to the stream," I rose and invited my sisters. Arm in arm, we strolled a small distance from the two warriors.

"We are glad you came to visit, Sabine," Muriel said.

"I wish you didn't have to go back," Fleur added.

A lump rose in my throat. I wondered if I could bargain for more time. My sisters seemed charmed by the warrior's careful manners. Thin civility, considering they were the ones that caused our captivity.

"I do also, but I am still needed."

"Oh we understand," Muriel waved a hand.

"You do?"

"Yes. You're lovers, aren't you?"

My mouth gaped.

"It's all right," Fleur continued. "We understand how you

healed them. The sooner they are better, the sooner we can be a family again."

"Though not in the village," Muriel said. "Perhaps we can live in a hut closer to the Berserkers."

Now I couldn't breathe for shock.

Fleur leaned in conspiratorially. "Muriel has an interest in one of the wolves. A young red one. He's not of this pack-- he was sneaking around here and is actually a spy for Brenna's pack...long story."

I was reeling. "You...have an interest in one of these brutes?"

"They're not brutes," Muriel defended.

Fleur winked at me.

"Anyway, your men are very beautiful," Muriel said after sticking her tongue out at her twin. Not so grown up, then.

"They're not my men..." I floundered.

"Then why do they look at you like you're the goddess incarnate? And you aren't unaffected either."

"I'm not in love. I can't be. They haven't allowed me to choose," I said.

"Perhaps you should ask Brenna." My sisters were in accord. "She has been living with them longer. She may know."

I started to protest again--my feelings for my Alphas, my sister's own outrageous ideas about our future--when a structure caught my eye. Tall as my shoulder, long and wide as two men, the frame was made of thick branches lashed together.

"What is that?"

"They caged us at first," Fleur said even as Muriel hushed her.

"What?" I hissed.

"Sabine," Maddox called. "You have walked long enough. It is time to return."

"It's all right, Sabine," Muriel said, catching my stiff arm. "We were fine."

"It was for our own safety. They let us out after they knew they could control themselves," Fleur explained hurriedly.

"Ladies," Ragnvald started to approach us. "Back to your tent. Your new guards arrive soon, and we need to get Sabine home before dusk."

"Yes, my lord," my sisters murmured, and hugged me goodbye. With worried looks when I didn't respond, they slipped away.

Teeth clenched, I marched to the cage and examined it. The Berserkers had fashioned the cage from stripped saplings and tree branches.

"You kept them in a cage?" I ground out, unwilling to face them.

"It was necessary," Maddox said at my back.

"We need to go," Ragnvald murmured. "It's been a long day, and my control..."

When Maddox took my arm, I wrenched it away.

"Don't touch me. Don't ever touch me again."

"Sabine, you heard your sister. It was for their protection."

"Protection they needed because of you!"

"We moved them to the tent after a night or two..." Again Maddox reached for my arm and I finally whirled to slap his hand away.

His hand shot out and shackled my wrist.

"Did you just strike me?"

"You kept my sisters in a cage!" I tried to slap him with

my free hand, and ended up struggling face to face with an enraged warrior.

Ragnvald sighed, but kept his distance. I felt his control fraying even as he said in a low voice, "You forget your place, little one."

"Punish me then," I snapped.

"Oh we shall." Maddox tossed me over his shoulder and slammed the breath from my lungs. Marching on past the cage and the stream, he broke into a trot that kept me hanging on to his belt for the brisk journey. Ragnvald did not follow right away. I wondered if he stayed away to regain his control.

Maddox did not swing me down until we were close to home. I felt the anger coming off him, a tense heat. Judging by the glow of his golden eyes, his beast was close to the surface.

"You are lucky we were not near the pack. You would already be strung up before them. Some might ask to take turns wielding the whip."

I struggled but Maddox easily overpowered and bound me, stretching my arms over my head by a rope hung from the branch of a tree. He laid his hands on my collar and with one move tore the beautiful overdress from my body.

"No," I cried, too late. He tossed the pieces into the woods.

"Yes. You'll be lucky if we allow you clothes for a sennight. We should keep you tied and docile in our bed, until you remember your place."

My curses rang out in the cool afternoon air.

"You think you are strong now. Wait until you've tasted the snake's bite."

He unwound a long strip of wide leather, cut thin with a

point at the end. My lip curled even as I shivered in my thin shift.

"Do your worst."

Mouth set, he held the end of the whip in one hand and the handle in the other. He popped it at my back, to the right of my spine, near my shoulder blade.

I gasped and twisted as if I could get away. The snap did nothing to warn me of the force of the leather and how one spot would burn like fire. The breath left my lungs and my mind filled with pain. My body jerked with the next stroke, and the next, and I almost lost my footing.

"No, please," I gasped. I could barely believe the pain in just a few strikes. I would not live through another.

"You want to beg now?" He lightly flogged my back through the shift. It didn't hurt, but my skin grew warm. "You want mercy?"

"Please--" I danced on tiptoe until Maddox came close and caught me.

"We will not allow you to endanger yourself in any way." There was no anger in his rawboned face, but no pity either. He moved back and I realized Ragnvald had caught up with us.

"We should just ban her from any more pack gatherings." Ragnvald said.

Now my lungs seized. If they did that, I would not see Brenna.

"No." I croaked. "Anything...I will submit to punishment." I gripped the rope with my hands holding my arms taut. I could hold on. "I will obey. Please punish me as you will."

With brisk hands, Maddox tucked my braid back over my shoulder. First he wielded a flogger made of braided strands ending in small rosebud knots. The blows warmed my back. As they grew heavier, I stifled my cries. When Maddox paused to rip off my shift, I let a sob of grief for losing the garment. Positioning my braid behind my back, Maddox painted my bare front pink. The strikes made me wince, but nothing like the brutal pain of the snake whip.

Ragnvald stayed at a distance while Maddox flowed in a dance of his own before me. His body tense as he concentrated on each blow. Watching the impressive muscles of his arm coil and strike with precision, I felt grateful that he wasn't using his full strength.

At a pause in the beating, Ragnvald came and ran a hand down my marked flesh.

"If any one of the pack had seen you attack us--even your sisters--I would not allow Maddox to be so gentle," Ragnvald said. "We would drag you back to the place of stones and string you up in front of the entire pack. And there would be no warm up. These first gentle lashes will allow Maddox to go longer, but you will feel less pain."

"Thank you, my lord."

His face remained impassive. "Continue," he told Maddox, who now held only the snake-tongued whip.

"Stay still, Sabine, or this will harm and not just hurt you."

The first pop made me gasp, the second choke. All the air rushed out of my lungs and I cried out in agony.

"Be still, Sabine." He was at my back now, snapping the whip at my shoulders, upper back. Each blow hit like a tree branch slammed into a place the size of a thumbprint, and drove my breath out of my body.

She does well, taking all that pain.

I almost turned my head to hear who had spoken before I realized it was in my head.

She will be rewarded. Somehow I knew the second voice was Ragnvald.

I breathed through the pop on my buttocks, but when the lash licked the sensitive skin of my thighs I began writhing again. Pain took me in its grip, and I lost myself to it, howling with tears streaming down my cheeks.

"Tell me, Sabine. Will you attack us again?"

"No, no," I sobbed.

"Will you submit to our will?"

"Anything. Please."

"A few more," Maddox said. "Give yourself over to the pain."

I shuddered as I nodded. I would try. I had no choice.

"One," Maddox counted, popping the whip against my right shoulder. "Two." The left.

I kept my place, pressing my face into my arms.

"Three." My right buttock. "Four." I bit into my own flesh and still cried out.

"Breathe, Sabine," Ragnvald ordered. Maddox waited until I obeyed.

I focused on my sisters, jerking through the lashes on my right thigh and left. Sagging, I prayed Maddox was done.

"Four more," he said, and it broke me. Chest heaving with hard sobs, I let myself hang in my bonds as he walked around to face me, a cold but not cruel expression on his face.

"Not her breasts, Maddox," Ragnvald said. "Keep to her back, this time."

Maddox acknowledged him with a bow. I tried to remember what they'd told me about punishment.

Ragnvald stayed across the clearing, watching me from there, and I realized this was for his benefit. I'd pushed the limits of his control, and without this ritual to put me in my place, he was unable to keep the beast from breaking free.

"Forgive me." I didn't realize I'd spoken until Maddox put his hand on my shoulder

"What was that?" Ragnvald asked, coming closer.

"Forgive me, Alpha. I was wrong. I didn't think and I put you--all of us in danger."

Ragnvald nodded to Maddox and he cut me down, catching me carefully. The tattooed warrior bathed my face with a wet cloth--remains of my shift, I thought ruefully.

"We don't want to hurt you," Ragnvald said. His eyes were back to a light blue. "This, at least, you can heal from."

"I understand," I croaked.

"You must learn," Maddox leaned in. "Or we cannot take you to the gathering."

"I will learn, I promise."

"Very well," Ragnvald said.

Maddox carried me to the cave, lay me down and fussed over me. Ragnvald held my hand as my marks were treated with salve.

"If you needed greater punishment, we would not treat your wounds for a day. If at all."

I brought his hand to my mouth and kissed his knuckles in gratitude.

"Sweet Sabine," he murmured. "You did so well."

"We will now give you a reward. A reminder of what lies in store when you behave," Maddox parted my legs gently, and held them open when I tried to close them.

"No, please--" I gulped down my protest.

"Do you deny us your pleasure?"

"No, no, my lord." I widened my legs, praying they would not punish me again.

"Calm yourself, Sabine. We are your masters. We may

not give you what you want, but we will always give what you need." His fingers thrummed between my legs, the slightest of touches.

"She's already slick," Maddox told Ragnvald.

"She's ready for us, but we will not take her tonight. She has given enough."

"Let us soothe you now." Maddox played with my fore and bottom hole awhile before brushing his finger against the sweet spot. I cried out as the dull throbbing in my whipped back turned into a happy ache. Maddox's fingers thrummed the right spot again and again, turning my body into a vessel of perfect agony. Pain was pleasure and pleasure was pain.

"Cum, Sabine," Ragnvald ordered, and I broke into a thousand pieces, writhing and panting on the pelts.

Maddox and Ragnvald watched me, and their satisfied looks sated me as much as the orgasm had.

Sleep claimed me, and as I sank into the darkness, I felt the men's contented presence, warm as a blanket where they lay at my side, and lay as shadows in my mind.

8

I woke groaning, my back on fire. Maddox stood over me in a second and I cringed away.

His hand soothed down my hip as he offered me a drink. "You have nothing to fear from me, Sabine. The beast desires your submission, nothing more."

He reapplied salve to my body, but I moved slowly that morning. The warriors seemed distant, though they treated me with utmost care and respect. I remained quiet, acting with careful deference. The marks would take some time to heal, but I didn't mind them so much as the thought that they would not bring me to see Brenna.

Later that day, Maddox brought me a blue gown to replace the one he'd torn.

"Should I wait to wear this? It is too fine a dress for everyday, but perhaps if we are going to the Thing."

"Wear it, Sabine," Maddox said. "We have trunkfuls of things coming for you and your sisters. And nothing is too fine for you."

I bit my lip and dressed. The gown set off my skin and flaxen hair perfectly.

Maddox's eyes lit when he saw me. He ran his finger along the collar of the gown and sent shivers all through me.

"Beautiful."

I waited for him to do more, but he only turned and walked away. A lump rose in my throat.

Ragnvald also liked the gown, judging by the soft kiss he gave me, but treated me with the same aloofness Maddox had. The warmth I'd felt last night was gone. The warriors were withdrawing from me.

At the fire that night, I finally worked up my nerve to speak.

"When do we go to the Gathering?" I asked.

"Soon," Ragnvald said. "We postponed it a few days."

"Is it--" I could barely get the words out. "Did I delay it?"

"No."

Yet the men continued to frown. After eating, Maddox left. Ragnvald stayed, staring into the fire. He hadn't touched his food at all.

Real fear rose in me. I served Ragnvald a bowl of stew and then knelt before him.

"I will submit to any term," I told him. "I will obey, I will wear the collar and chain and crawl if I must."

"That is not necessary."

"Please, just give me a command. I will prove I can obey."

Setting aside the food, he drew me into his lap. "You accepted punishment. It's over. You are forgiven. That is the way of the pack."

"Then what is wrong?"

"Negotiations are delayed. Brenna's pack does not trust us. The last time we had a Gathering, our pack attacked them. I was not fully in control, and neither was Maddox, though he led the raid. We were desperate men, desperate for anything that would save us."

"What will be done?"

"They ask for a gesture of goodwill. A hostage. Someone to trade."

"Who?"

"Me," Maddox strode from the forest. "It is done, Alpha. Their emissary arrived and bore witness that Sabine's twin sisters are being well treated. One of them will remain as their guard. The rest will take me and return to their mountain."

I stood, ready to run from him, but the sight of a silent line of strange warriors emerging from the trees brought me up short. Forgetting the rules of the pack, I stared at them. They looked better fed and rested than Ragnvald's men, but all were large and brutal looking. One warrior, a giant with a shaven head, bore a scar slashing across his face. He caught me staring, and I remembered to drop my eyes.

Maddox opened his arms and I stepped into their protection.

"Are they from Brenna's pack?" I didn't ask if she was with them. Booted and bearing arms, the warriors carried no packs, nothing beyond their blades.

"They wanted to see that you are healthy, Sabine. And I wanted to say goodbye."

Ragnvald greeted the warriors while I clung to Maddox.

"How long will you be gone?" I spoke in a low voice, keeping our words between us.

"Until after the Gathering." His finger stroked my lips. "Heed Ragnvald and be good."

I couldn't quite joke with him. So much was riding on the truce between the packs. "I will." My lip trembled under his touch.

"Will you miss me, little witch?"

"No." But my hands cupped his face, tracing the harsh lines of his jaw and cheekbones, memorizing the stark beauty I hadn't seen there, not at first. "Will they be cruel to you?"

"Perhaps. I deserve it. I was cruel to you."

"Not always. Sometimes you were kind." Ragnvald and the other warriors had finished their business and were watching us.

I wanted to ask if there was a chance that he might not return.

"Those men...they look ready to spill blood."

"There is danger," Maddox said as if he read my thoughts. "but I will return to you." He hugged me close. "I swear it.

"You don't have to do this," I whispered against his chest. "I don't want you to."

"Sometimes, we take a chance for the ones we love."

He squeezed my hand and stepped away. My arm stretched after him as if its intent was to keep hold until the last.

Before he could let go, I gripped him hard and pulled him back. In the sight of all the enemy, I kissed Maddox, twining my hands in his dark hair. Tattooed arms rising to lock me against him, he took over, slanting my head back so he could plunder what already belonged to him.

A lifetime later--though it was but a moment, Ragnvald stood beside us clearing his throat. I let him draw me away while Maddox loped off, shooting a heated glance or two backwards before the strange warriors closed ranks behind him. They herded him off, the giant scarred one waiting to bring up the rear.

I didn't bother to hide my glare in his direction. The

scarred face almost broke into a smile before he too, turned and followed the others into the trees.

～

The waiting began. I tried to hide it but I was sick with worry. The grimness in Ragnvald's mood didn't lessen. He stayed close to me, unspeaking, hovering like a bodyguard. At times I caught him grimacing as if he was in pain. He hid it from me, and didn't otherwise seem sick, so I didn't mention the matter.

Ragnvald and I fucked every night, with quiet, desperate movements. Afterwards, I draped my body over his long one, and we lay entwined like that for long sleepless hours.

At last word came. With Maddox in their custody, Brenna's Alphas agreed to set the Gathering a week hence.

Ragnvald wouldn't allow me out of his sight, so I accompanied him on all pack business. I grew used to wearing the collar and chain, but before long, Ragnvald dispensed with the walk to the standing stones, and held his audiences at our cave. In the informal setting I was allowed to do my work, as long as the pack respected my space and I did not overtly challenge them.

I was browsing for herbs at the river bank, when I had a visitor of my own--a woman in a simple green gown, that somehow shimmered in the early morning light. "So this is the great Ragnvald's consort," she murmured, almost to herself.

Ragnvald's voice still echoed through the trees; he was close enough to call in case of danger. The lady bore no weapon that I could see, though something about her haughty calm told me she wasn't defenseless.

"Hello, little...what does he call you? Little witch?"

I realized I was stroking the torc around my neck and dropped my hand. "Maddox is the only one who calls me that."

"And are you?"

"Am I what?"

"A witch?"

"No." I gave up on courtesy. The woman had none. "Why? Are you?"

She smiled, and it was more frightening than friendly. "Yes." The woman laughed at my expression.

I looked for Ragnvald and the warriors he'd been meeting with, but the bushes seemed to have grown up around us.

"Just us, dearie," the woman purred. "But if you prefer..." She waved a hand and I heard voices wafting on the breeze. Ragnvald sounded as if he was only a few feet away.

"He isn't far. And he trusts me."

"Who are you?" I asked, jealously like acid in my belly. She was beautiful in a cold, otherworldly way. Like a storm in the distance, or an eagle to an ant. I did not like feeling that I was the ant.

" I am Yseult. Come." She sat on a boulder and patted the rock beside her. "I wish to speak to you. You seem much more interesting than your sister."

I sat. "Which one?"

"Brenna, of course."

"You've seen her?"

"My dear, I'm the one who told the Berserkers about her."

I sucked in a breath. "You told the prophecy."

"I cast runes. Yes. I told Brenna's mates about her. I was not the one to first tell Maddox and Ragnvald of your existence, but I may have taken pity on them and told them where to find you."

My world narrowed on the lovely woman before me. Here was my true enemy. I should feel angry, and yet everything in me wanted to fawn over her beauty and serve her. I gripped the stem in my hand until the thorns broke my skin. The pain cleared my head.

Yseult's glance at my fist told me she didn't miss the motion. Her smile told me she approved.

"So I have you to thank for ruining my life," I said.

"For ruining your life? No. For finding your destiny, yes. You may thank me."

"You don't know this is my destiny."

"Neither do you. Unless you will admit to having power."

"The Berserkers think I have some," I said carefully.

"A bit more than some. But a lot less than me."

Just like that, I'd had enough of her preening.

"My sister and I have the power to heal the Berserkers."

"Your sisters are spaewives. Not so rare a race, but few know what they are. You pass for a normal human and have affinity for herbs and healing. It's a deeper, subtler magic."

"We go into heat at the time of the moon."

"Oh yes, the estrous. That is a response to the Berserkers, I believe. It grows stronger the longer you deny it, calling to your true mates until they come and claim you."

I huffed.

"You do not believe me?"

"I know it is true," I sighed.

"You wish it wasn't."

I didn't deny it.

"I have a theory." Yseult settled beside me, tucking her feet up under her skirts like we were girls talking of the midsummer market, not a witch and a Berserker consort speaking of magic. "The beast that feeds off the Berserker rage, it enjoys lust. There is the wolf, you see, and that is natural, at peace, as long as it has its pack and place within it. Then there is the man. Men can be ruled by all sorts of passions, but these warriors can control those. What they can't control is the beast."

"What is the beast?"

"Hunger. Thirst. Pure wanting. Much like you experience during the full of the moon."

I stayed silent.

"Imagine that agony, but every day. Multiply it a thousand times, and stretch it across a century."

I fought the urge to hide my face in my skirts. "I cannot comprehend it."

"Of course not. Neither can they. That is why they go mad."

"But that can't happen any more, right?"

"Not if you don't keep yourself from them. Your moon lust and their moon madness..." She laced her fingers together.

"We fit. I know."

"Then why are you fighting it?"

"Did they ask you to speak to me?"

"Your Alphas? No. But only because they are afraid to let you near me." Her smile was terrifying.

"Are you such a threat?" I kept my voice light.

"Of course I am, but not to you. I just told you--I find you interesting. That is why your men wouldn't want us meeting. I don't want to harm you. I want to teach you."

She left me speechless for a moment. "Why?"

Her slender fingers toyed with my hair, much like Maddox often did. Both acted as if they owned me, but where his touch was admiring, hers was condescending, like I was a pretty pet who amused her for the moment. "Real women of power are so hard to come by."

I rose from the rock, to stop her from touching me. "I do not have so much power."

"Not yet. You won't even embrace your destiny."

"This is not my destiny." I waved at the forest, and the cave.

"Oh, and what is? Squatting in a human village, waiting for the day a priest realizes your influence upstages his, and decides you must burn? Will you marry some brute for his protection? Bear his children, his beatings until he dies and you're driven to drink? That was your mother's life."

A fist clenched around my heart. "I make my own path."

"Do you? You are not free from the ties that bind each of us to the other...any more than I am. Freedom is an illusion."

"My grandmother was free."

"Yes, and she died. A vagabond and alone."

"You'd have me stay and consort with these men?" I kept my tone level. It wouldn't be wise to offend a woman of this power, but I wanted to slap her. As much as I wished to air my thoughts and confused feelings, I didn't want a witch meddling. I'd hoped to speak of this with Brenna, after all, she had been living as a captive of the Berserkers all this time. "You say you want to teach me. Why?"

"Power begets power."

I leveled a stare at the witch, careful to focus on her face and not her eyes in case she could ensnare me that way.

Yseult sighed, guessing that I would not speak until she gave me a better answer. "There is a war coming only Berserkers can fight, and there is a role I must play in it. I will need all the help I can get."

I ignored the prickle down my spine at her words. She spoke the truth, and my instinct confirmed it.

"If you stay, you will grow your power. Already, you are stronger. Your moon lust will temper theirs."

I frowned, thinking it was true.

"And then there's the punishments." Yseult licked her lips. "Your mates' pretty whips and chains."

I stiffened. "What of those?" I felt mortified that she knew of those things.

"Why, pain makes magic stronger. Haven't you noticed?"

I hadn't, so said nothing.

"All magic requires sacrifice to satisfy the gods. A witch like myself only needs a little pain. A sparrow, a mouse, a goat here and there."

My gut twisted. She was speaking of animal sacrifice, and not a quick clean death. Torture.

"There's human sacrifice--but only the darkest arts require that."

"My sisters and I would never--"

"I know, I know," Yseult waved a hand. "Hedge witches like you and your sister are a different breed. Your pain and sacrifice comes from a different source."

"What source?"

"Yourself. You submit yourself to pain. That is why these Berserkers worship you. Their beast lusts for violence. In times of war they will subdue armies. In times of peace--"

"They will subdue me," I finished dryly. We didn't need to speak of all the ways Maddox and Ragnvald had subdued me in our short time together. Or how I'd enjoyed it--begged for it, even.

Yseult inclined her head.

"And my submission brings power?"

"Your submission is power. But yes. One packet of your herbs would heal a village, now."

Her eyes were strange, yellow with a green band. I wondered that I'd ever thought her human.

"Why are you telling me this?"

"I wish to help."

"I want to go home."

"Then ask. These wolves will give you anything."

Anything, they'd said in my dream, *but that.*

"Don't you know, Sabine?" Yseult rose and walked to me, a sway in her hips that left my mouth dry. I'd never desired a woman before, but this one stirred forbidden feelings...of many kinds. "They're more than a little in love with you."

"I wish that things could go back to the way they were before." I hated the tangled mess. The pack politics were even more deadly and dangerous than human ones.

There is a war coming only Berserkers can fight, and there is a role I must play in it.

"Do you?" Yseult wrapped one hand around my shoulder. I didn't dare pull away.

"Your power grows stronger...so tasty. No wonder these warrior wolves can't get enough."

Her nails bit into my skin, waking me up as the thorns had.

I blinked, and the spell was broken. Ordinary eyes stared out of an ordinary face. Yseult and I looked alike, I realized. Blonde hair and hazel eyes, while all my sisters had darker hair.

I stepped back.

"I will heal Ragnvald and the pack. That is all they asked for. Then my sisters and I will return to the village and live as we have always done."

AFTER THE WITCH LEFT, I sat and stared into the fire for a long time.

"Sabine?"

A rustle behind me, but I didn't move even when Ragnvald's hand came to my shoulder. I flinched, but there was no pain from Yseult's original grip. I'd checked for broken skin, and found none.

"Sabine, are you alright?"

I nodded and submitted to his perusal.

"I did not know she had come to you first. She told me before she disappeared." He finished checking me over and sounded relieved. Lifting me in his arms, he carried me back to the cave.

He fed the fire, then came to my back, sat and wrapped his arms around me. He didn't speak until I relaxed against his chest.

"What did you and Yseult speak of?"

"Magic. Power."

His laugh gusted at my ear. "She loves to speak of those things."

"She said my power is growing. That witches like her make sacrifices to the gods, but I am my own sacrifice."

"You have sacrificed much for us. We are forever in your debt."

Twisting in his lap, I faced him.

"Are we safe?"

"From Brenna's pack? Or from the beast within?" Ragnvald went on before I could find a way to tell him I worried about both. "My beast is all but tamed, little one. And Brenna's pack--we walk an uneasy path, but it leads to peace."

I laid my hand on the perfect plane of his cheek, beautiful and pale as if carved from marble by the gods.

Yseult spoke of a war only the Berserkers could win, that she would play a part in. If I chose not to accept my place as my Alpha's mate, did she mean to suggest they would not win?

Either way, if I left, I had to resign myself to losing these men, one way, or another. It is one thing to lay love aside, and another to lose it forever.

Unable to look at the Viking's beauty any longer, I settled back in his arms, and let him simply hold me.

"Do you think he's safe?"

Ragnvald sighed. "He is not comfortable, but he is alive. Can you not feel him?"

I closed my eyes, and when I focused, a presence stirred in my heart. Like my knowledge that Brenna was alive, but stronger.

Maddox, I thought, and the presence grew stronger. *Yseult says I have powers.*

I could almost see his grin. *Told you, little witch.*

A breeze blew over the fire, making the ashes dance. Together Ragnvald and I watched them rise against the moon. We didn't move. On this night, we both needed comfort.

"I miss him."

9

It took a day for us to trek to the Thing, and would've taken longer, but once I grew tired, Ragnvald swung me up in his arms and ran. As the forest flew by, I caught glimpses of warriors on either side of us, carrying axes and spears and traveling as fast as we were. When Ragnvald stopped, they formed a loose circle around us. Most were barechested and only wearing leather breeches. A few had wolf pelts slung over their shoulders. Some were in wolf form.

I kept my eyes down and waited for Ragnvald to leash me, but he only took a strip of leather and wound it around my wrist. "These wolves are more civilized," he told me. "And so is our pack now, thanks to you."

He held the end of the leather thong tying my wrist, so I was still leashed, but it wasn't as humiliating.

"The other rules still apply," he warned, and I nodded, eager to prove that I could behave. One act of defiance, one slip, and I might destroy the uneasy peace between packs.

Ragnvald led me to a clearing with standing stones, much like the one his men had made by the seaside. Each stone was twice as tall as I was, and thrice as thick. Passing under a gate made of three stone slabs, I realized the Berserkers made these formations. The stones would stand for centuries, a testament to the pack's unworldly strength.

The other pack waited for us by a bonfire in the center of the stone circle. The flames cast shadows on their faces. The moon also lent her silvery light.

An oppressive feeling rolled over me as we faced the enemy pack, as if the bad blood between the packs weighed the air.

I followed behind Ragnvald, in a tight knot of warriors. Three enemy warriors moved out of the mass of grim wolves to greet us.

In the heavy silence, Ragnvald stopped a few feet from the approaching triangle. They seemed to be waiting for something. No one spoke. My body was so tense one touch would make it snap. If the opposing pack attacked, we would all surely die.

With a nod to the three leaders, Ragnvald stepped away, revealing me to their pack.

Immediately the choking gravity lessened, and I could breathe again. I stiffened my spine as every wolf in the clearing studied me. The foremost enemy warrior, pale-skinned and blond much like Ragnvald, though much broader and not as tall, stepped forward, a friendlier look on his bearded face.

"Well met, Ragnvald of Norway."

∼

THE FIRST ROUND of discussion at the Gathering ended soon after moonrise. Brenna's Berserkers didn't speak directly to me.

"Out of respect to me," Ragnvald told me as soon as we'd left the place of stones. "Tomorrow, we will meet in private with the Alphas, and be less formal. They will allow you to see Brenna then. From what I know, she is well, but her mates are very protective."

"Mates?"

"The two Alphas we met."

"The blond and the dark haired one?" I guessed. The third leader had been the scar-faced warrior with the shaved head. Wulfgar, they called him. He was a Viking like Ragnvald, like most of the wolves, besides Maddox.

Wulfgar was the one who led us to the lodging where Ragnvald and I could spend the night. The rest of the pack had their own bonfire. The light flickered through the trees, and as we approached the tent, I heard a happy clamor--a toast of some sort.

"Your hospitality is well received," Ragnvald said to Wulfgar.

The scarred hulk smiled. "We welcome those who come in peace."

"Tonight we drink to peace; tomorrow we'll pledge to it."

Wulfgar merely inclined his head.

A fine woven rug ran between two torches, leading us to the tent door. Before I could enter, Maddox stepped out.

His face looked leaner, the eyes more shadowed, but his body strong and easily able to catch my weight when I ran and leapt into his arms. As Maddox carried me inside and let the tent flap fall, I heard Ragnvald chuckling behind us.

Inside Maddox kissed me with such passion, I was sure tomorrow I would have bruises.

"Please," I said, already struggling out of my fine gown. It wouldn't do for it to be ripped on the morrow, but I had to touch him, press my naked flesh against him.

We came together as soon as Maddox stripped off his breeches.

Maddox's fingers bit into my hips as he positioned me where he wanted me. "Sabine, I want... I can't be gentle--"

"Don't be--" I surged up to take his lips, and gasped as his cock speared me. My legs hooked around his back, forcing him in faster, my body stretching around him, welcoming the burn.

Afterward, I lay in his arms, tracing the pattern of his tattoos, memorizing their shadowed depths.

"When did you get these?" I asked, stroking his inked skin. "I thought Berserker's bodies healed quickly. Did you get them before or after you were...changed?"

"I fell asleep under the curse, and when I woke, I was marked."

He seemed content to lie under me and accept my soothing touch. The bruises under his eyes had grown lighter. I wondered what scars his fast-healing skin hid.

"Did they hurt you?" We hadn't yet spoken of the other Berserker pack.

"Nothing permanent. They took their debt out of my hide but it was not so much that I couldn't bear it."

I remembered Ragnvald's pained looks around the fire. "Ragnvald took the pain for you, didn't he?"

Maddox's silence gave me my answer.

Laying my head on his chest, I sucked in a breath against angry tears. "I should've never have let them take you."

His hand stroked my hair. "I would've gone anyway. You couldn't have stopped me. Truth was, they were gentler than they would've been if they hadn't seen us kiss. Admit it, witch, you care for me.

"Wolf." I sharpened my tone but couldn't quite mean it. "You forget your place."

"As do you," he found the leather strip that Ragnvald had used to leash me, and wound it over his palm until I was tethered tightly to him. "Beneath me, attending to my cock."

I rolled my eyes and just like that, my tears were gone.

"You also helped me," he continued in a more serious tone.

"When?"

"When you reached out to me. I heard you," he tapped his temple. "Here. That and knowing you were waiting and missing me...I could've survived any torture."

"You really heard me?"

He nodded.

"So we share a bond? Is that even possible between a woman and a wolf?"

"Not just any woman." He rolled and now I was underneath him, enjoying the rippling muscles in his arms as they held him over me. "I have learned much from these Berserkers. The moon goddess looked down on the earth and saw her children--the wolves--were breeding too slowly to replenish their packs. She gave the spell of the Change to her priestesses, but the magic was used for ill and became tainted. So she set her magic deep inside the most devoted priestesses, pure of heart. They can mate with wolves, and can tame the beast."

"Spaewives," I said.

"Yes. They are the most beautiful, most gentle of women. Docile, submissive, obedient."

"You should find one of these women, then," I said tartly, pushing at his shoulders. "She will make you and Ragnvald the most marvelous mate."

He laughed and didn't let me get away, but held me down and did...other things. Ragnvald came in from toasting at the bonfire, and added his own drunken revelry to our mix. The sky was grey with dawn before we'd sated ourselves with each other and lay in a tangle, dozing.

"We will not search for any other," Maddox nuzzled my neck. "We have the one we want, right here."

∽

THE THREE OF us went to meet Brenna and her mates, holding hands. I felt a little nervous walking up the mountain path, but it could've been the scrutiny of all the assembled wolves. The mountain Berserkers had posted guards three deep outside the cavern where we were to meet.

"Last time we came to see Brenna, we were going to steal her," Maddox murmured. Neither he nor Ragnvald seemed to mind the glares of the other pack. Or if they did, the Alphas didn't show it.

I gave them a sharp look, and Maddox grimaced. "We were desperate, little witch."

"Things have changed." With a hand on my back, Ragnvald guided me into the cavern. Two great warriors--the two foreign Alphas I recognized from the Gathering last night--waited for us. One sat on rock carved to look like a throne. The other stood as a guard, a hand resting on his weapon. There was no one else.

Fear seized me for a moment--could this be an ambush? I felt my two Alphas stiffen beside me, but a woman stepped out from behind the throne--tall, dark haired, with serene features and the scar at her throat. Brenna.

I couldn't stop from running to her, or she to me. Protocol be damned.

Luckily, the two sets of warriors moved away.

Tears squeezed from my eyes as I hugged her. She

smelled of earth and spice, the mountain and her own familiar scent.

"I knew you were alive," I whispered in her ear and she drew back to kiss my cheek.

I realized I felt her belly between us. We broke apart and I studied her lush form. I'd been so eager to see my sister, I hadn't noticed it at first.

"Pregnant?" I spoke with my hands, using the private language we'd invented as children, after the wolf attack took her voice.

"Yes." she signed back. "My mates." Flushing, she nodded to the two warriors at her back. To my surprise, they both bowed to me.

My own warriors moved close enough I felt their heat.

"How can this be?" Ragnvald asked with naked eagerness in his voice.

"The spaewives can mate with wolves fully," Daegan said.

"Whether they bear humans or pups remains to be seen," Samuel said and I detected a tinge of worry in his voice, not that he'd show such weakness to us.

Brenna's wide smile belied any fear. Her mates came forward and kissed her, one by one, before moving to greet my Alphas.

I swallowed the lump in my throat.

"Are you well?" My voice wobbled on the last word.

More than well. She signed back. *I am happy.*

∽

Brenna's mates made us as welcome as they could. After greetings, they led us to another cavern carved deep in the mountain, with a long table laid out for a feast. Ragnvald and Samuel claimed the most dominant position at the opposing heads of table, while Maddox and Daegan ranged about the room like guards. Sitting side by side in the middle of the table, Brenna and I ignored them.

What happened when you were taken? I asked in our secret sign language.

Fear at first, but they were kind to me.

The more I studied my sister, the more I realized the glow of her cheeks and sparkle in her eyes wasn't just from the baby she carried. She'd told me from the first: she was happy. What's more, she was in love with these men. She thrived here, in their care.

After hearing my story, Brenna asked after the twins. She already knew our mother and stepfather were dead.

My men told me, she said. *They shelter me, but do not hide the truth. At least, not for long.* She smiled, a secret smile echoed on the faces of her lovers.

Sabine, what's wrong?

"I'm so glad to know you're alive. I missed you," I choked out.

Brenna laid a hand on my leg, and I knew I didn't have her fooled. Cold silence encased me, though I forced a smile to my face. I hadn't realized how much I'd hoped for an ally amid the Berserkers.

I waited until the meal ended, and the warriors went to one side of the room to talk, leaving us in a semblance of privacy.

"I don't understand," I said at last. "How can you be happy here?"

I am alive for a reason. A purpose. She touched the scar at her throat, and my gut clenched in shock. Brenna never acknowledged the reminder of her wounds, of the attack. *I was waiting for my purpose. I was waiting for them.*

She looked so content I averted my gaze and stared into the fire.

"They kidnapped me," I started listing their sins, and Brenna cut me off with a wave.

Our stepfather sold me. Brenna signed. *Before that, he abused me. I made sure he would never hurt you the same way.*

In that moment I knew she had asked for his death, and the Berserkers had carried it out.

They have given me everything I asked for, and more." Her movements were graceful and flowing and passionate.

"You could've come back, and been with us."

I made a vow to stay. She paused and shook her head. *Even if I could leave, I would not.*

"Why?"

I'm in love. She took my hand and squeezed it, forcing me to stay facing her.

Sabine. After all we've been through, is it so frightening to fall in love?

10

I stayed quiet on the journey home. The men let me be, after giving me reassurance that all my sisters would be reunited again. They thought I grieved our parting, but I was relieved. I'd expected an ally in my anger, in my war against my feelings. But it was Brenna's way to accept her lot in life and make it better. It's what gave her such a deep peace.

My own thoughts were in turmoil.

As we neared the cave, I stopped in my tracks.

"Sabine? Is something wrong?"

"Take it off," I clawed at the silver at my throat. Brenna wore a similar torc, and her men wore arm rings that pledged themselves to her. "Take it off, please."

I was a fool, so stupid. I'd thought if I bargained, if I was clear, I could escape one day. But these Berserkers had searched for their mates for over a century. They would want children, and once they bred me, there would be no escape.

"Sabine?"

My fingers tore at the torc. "Take it off. Take it off. I don't want it anymore."

Maddox caught my hands and Ragnvald undid it.

My breath rasped painfully through my tight chest.

'I'm sorry," I said to both of them, my vision blurred. "I can't do this."

"Calm yourself," they said. "We are not brutes. You can talk to us."

"You don't understand. She was supposed to help me hate you," I raged, and felt them draw back. "I wasn't supposed to...You want me to be something I'm not. I never agreed to be your mate. To have children...To stay forever..." I scrubbed at my eyes until I could see their somber faces. "I did this to help you. Out of pity. No more."

"Sabine--"

Ragnvald held up a hand and Maddox subsided. "You truly feel nothing for us?"

"I--I don't know what I feel. But I don't want this." I waved my hand at the cave. "I wanted to chose my own path. I wanted to live my own life." The image of Brenna, rounded with child between her two Alphas, rose in my mind and wished I could wrench it from me as easily as the torc.

"You can't keep me here," I spoke to the ground.

"We can. But we won't, if you don't want to stay," Ragnvald said.

Maddox might have turned to stone for all the emotion he showed. So I railed at him.

"You tore me from my life. I was making my own way. I never would've known you. I never would've wanted you." My stomach clutched at his hurt expression. "I cannot give in to you without losing myself."

He turned away, and kept walking even when I called after him.

"I'm sorry, Maddox, please." I sank to the ground.

Ragnvald carried me back to the cave and laid me on the bed where I let myself weep for the Sabine who always walked a careful path and never left the boundaries drawn in her heart. That girl was dead and gone, and I was alone, without my vows to shield me.

"I want to go back." I spoke after an afternoon in the cave, tense and silent, waiting for the storm to pass.

Ragnvald sighed. "I gave you my word. I will not keep you."

"My sisters--"

"They must stay. They will be given to Berserkers as mates."

"You would give two young girls to the whole pack?" I whispered in shock.

"No, there will be a great competition, games for any warrior to compete for their hand in marriage. To the winners go the spoils."

"Spoils? You mean my sisters," I said with the sharp edge of temper.

"It cannot be helped, Sabine. It is part of the pact we made with Brenna's Alphas, but even if it were our decision alone...the life that Brenna has with her mates gives our pack too much to hope. We never thought we could live as men. We never thought..." Wonder warred with sorrow on the Alpha's face. I felt his struggle to put these feelings into words. "You have given us reason to come out of the cave."

I was waiting for my purpose, Brenna had said, an echo of Maddox and Yseult. *Your destiny.*

Summoning my selfishness, I asked, "What about me? Did you discuss my fate with the entire Thing, or just the Alphas and your pack?"

Ragnvald's voice was just as sharp as mine. "You belong to us, and to us alone. If we say you may go, you may go."

Rising, I walked to the edge of the cave and stopped short, as if I still wore a chain.

"It is for you to choose," Ragnvald finished.

I bit my lip. Could I really leave my sisters behind?

"What do you want, Sabine?" Maddox spoke from the shadows. His harsh voice told me he barely had control of his beast.

"I want my life back. I want to be free."

He stalked forward, shoulders hunched as if ready to drop into wolf form and hunt me like prey.

"Freedom, little witch? You'd leave us in slavery?"

"I saved you from the beast--"

"And yet we are all still chained. By you. To you. And you to us. Because we love, we will never be free."

"I will not ever love you," I spat.

Maddox's hand collared my throat.

"Maddox, step away," Ragnvald warned.

The gold in the tattooed warrior's eyes told me his beast was close. I waited for him to call me on the lie, but he only dropped his hand. "Then leave. There is nothing for you here."

∽

I CRIED a little as I packed my belongings, but did not waver.

"I'm ready," I told Ragnvald and he rose from the fire. Maddox had disappeared again.

"I'll escort you as far as I can. Beyond that, it will be safe for you to walk. The Berserkers are the most feared beasts on this island, and you carry our scent."

We walked in silence to the edge of Berserker territory. I

thought of all the things I could say, but in the end nothing would explain my selfishness. I wondered if I would ever see my sisters again. A part of me didn't care. Leaving felt like chopping off a limb. My mind and heart ached with a deeper pain.

I perked up when we came to a hill overlooking land that I recognized. Ragnvald stopped.

"There is the road," He pointed out the well travelled route. "This is as far as I go."

"Tell Maddox..." I forced words out. "Tell him I said goodbye."

Ragnvald paused as if waiting for me to say more. When I didn't, he sighed and rubbed the back of his neck, looking less like the Viking conqueror and more like a boy grown too tall too soon. "He didn't want to take you."

"What?"

"The pack forced him to do it. He took you for their sake, and for mine. If it were up to him, he would've happily died, rather than encroach upon your life and freedom." He said it without judgment, but I felt the weight of his words all the same.

He drew me into a hard hug.

"Go home, Sabine." His thumb brushed my lips, and when he stepped back, he wore the cold confidence of a ruler once more.

∼

I WENT HOME. The hut stank of old smoke and rushes, and was full of dried leaves. I spent the first few days cleaning it out, along with my garden. Most of my herbs were dead, as if it were my presence, not just the earth, sun, and rain, that made them thrive.

I avoided the village, and, though I foraged for food in the woods, I did not return to the grove.

On the third night, I returned from a long day searching for food and found gifts on my front stoop: three dead partridges and wood for the fire. I searched but couldn't find any trace of a visitor until the next night, when I caught sight of a dark wolf slipping between the trees along the path.

"No," I snapped and used my walking stick to shake the brush. "Maddox. Come out."

A wind lifted my hair and sent prickles down my spine. Maddox stepped out, clad only in a loin cloth, his tattoos displayed to their full glory.

My body ached at the sight, before I remembered I couldn't allow myself to want him.

"What are you doing here?" I made my voice harsh.

He stared at me a moment and I remembered it took a while for speech to return. He'd probably been living as a wolf for days.

"You need to leave," I said. "I've made my choice. I don't want you."

When he finally could speak, I could barely understand his rasping voice, "You think you chose freedom. It's not so simple."

"Of course it is. You came and ruined my life. Now you leave and let me be." My hands made a shooing motion and I squawked when he caught them in an iron grip. I fought but he drew me closer until I smelled his wild, perfect scent and stopped struggling.

"And what of the men that look at you? What about the priest that wants your death? He cannot control your power and cannot allow something stronger than his faith to exist." Maddox shook me. "Who will protect you when they come with rope to bind you and torches for the fire? I will not stand by and see you raped by men who cannot possess you. Not to mention my own pack--" He broke off with a ragged whine.

"Your own pack...what?"

This time he took a step back, his head bowed. "They threatened to bring you back again. Ragnvald can control them, but I will stay with you, and kill any who tries to break our vow to set you free."

"I'm sorry." Could I ever say those words enough to atone for my selfishness? "I must be true to myself."

"I understand." He dropped my hands. "I renounced the pack and will watch over you for the rest of my life."

"But you are a wolf. Without the pack...you will die."

He still stood close to me and I couldn't stop myself. I touched his jaw, finally noticing the deep shadows, the lines of strain in the cliffs and hollows of his perfect face. Maddox closed his eyes as if my touch both burned and soothed him, at the same time.

"Yes. I give you your freedom." He jerked backwards, away from me. "It is all you will allow me to give."

Before he loped into the forest, I ran after him. "Maddox--wait. Ragnvald told me you didn't want to take me at first. Is it true?"

"It is. I was going to let him die, let us all die. You were innocent. You had done nothing to deserve the cursed life that we live. The pack threatened to come for you. They would've taken you anyway, and my intentions would've been for nothing."

I bridged the distance between us and caught his arm. "Why didn't you tell me?"

His shoulders heaved with strain. "Would it have made a difference? I made the final decision to take you. I did not care that it was against your will. I hardened myself so I would not care."

Liar. I wanted to say. "Why did you come for me yourself?"

He lost--or won--the battle with his beast and turned fully to me. "Because I couldn't allow another to touch you. Sabine--" He did not kiss me, but everywhere his fingers skimmed left a trail of fire. Desire poured into me, taking over.

"No," I wrenched myself away. "I cannot do this." Retreating to my hut, I closed the door before he could follow.

I did not ask for this, I told myself fiercely. I had a right to my freedom.

"Besides," I muttered to myself, pacing in front of a cold fire. "Love makes a woman weak."

Night fell, and with it, the rain. I couldn't forget the image of a midnight wolf standing on the far side of the path, guarding the hut, eyes half closed against the wind.

Love makes a man weak.

When dawn broke I marched out. I hadn't eaten or slept, and neither had the wolf, for he raised his head immediately when I walked to him, walking stick in one hand, bag of herbs in the other.

"Take me to Ragnvald."

11

The Alpha sat at the fire at the mouth of the cave, half in and half out of shadow. He looked up as if'd I'd only stepped away for a moment. My whole body ached from my long pilgrimage, but I welcomed the pain.

"I want a house," I said. "My own dwelling with doors I can shut. Any who wish to enter must knock and I will choose when I will let them in."

"I suppose we can do all that." Ragnvald said.

"Thank you." A slight breeze ruffled his hair and mine, as if the forest sighed.

When I glanced back, Maddox stood there as a man. The magic of the Change left a leather loincloth around his waist, and a pelt across his shoulders. He looked gaunt and hungry, and I felt guilty because I had done this to him.

"He may not be able to speak for a while, but the pack bonds are restored," Ragnvald said.

I took the blond leader's hand, and held out my other to the tattooed warrior. Maddox kissed my fingers and a shiver went through me.

Our minds are linked, Maddox said clearly, though I didn't hear him with my ears. *The mating bond is complete. I know not when it happened.*

"I think," I said. "It was always there. You knew didn't you?" Maddox's smile showed his canines. "I heard you from the first. We always had the bond; it was just waiting for me."

I placed Ragnvald's hand on my hip before I turned to Maddox. "You would've given your life for me."

Gladly. His hand fisted my hair and released a second later. He found his voice. "I would die a thousand deaths before I hurt you."

I touched his face in wonder that such a man could exist.

Behind me, Ragnvald stood and pressed himself to my back.

"Stay with us, little witch. It does not have to be forever."

I smiled and turned so I touched both Maddox and Ragnvald at the same time. "Liar."

They lifted me between them, every movement in sync. I let them strip me and lay me down, and I touched them as much as I could before they bound my hands behind my back and fetched the whip.

"For leaving us," Ragnvald said, and held me as Maddox struck my breasts, again and again. I cried out and accepted the pain, feeling the bond between us open wider with each blow. With clever fingers between my folds, Ragnvald drove away the ache with rising pleasure. When my orgasm crested through me, Maddox looped the leather around my neck and pulled me forward, on top of him. His cocked speared me easily, and I rode him with only the wet smacking sound of my arousal between us.

"You realize that you can't go back now," Maddox's hands caught my hips with bruising force. "I don't care what

Ragnvald says. You try to escape and I will drag you back by your hair."

"You can try, wolf," I showed him my teeth. He slammed into me, brutal thrusts that had me crying out. I howled louder when Maddox slowed.

"Still, Sabine." The men tipped me forward and Ragnvald eased open my nether hole with a finger coated with oil.

"Then we will take you completely, and ruin you for any other," Ragnvald said, finger fucking my back hole. I felt full, so deliciously full with Maddox still inside. "You will never want to leave."

Grunting, I pushed back onto his fingers as he added a second, a third, and finally set his cock at my back star. The burn as he pushed in melded with the raw sting in my front. I cried out and their hands cradled me.

"Give us your pain, sweet one," Ragnvald whispered. As Maddox surged up to kiss me, I felt the bond open further, and the sharp sting disappeared, washed away in the current linking us. As I lay open between them, I felt a gentle throbbing--but I did not know if it hurt or felt good. It grew in intensity and I clawed at Maddox's shoulder in a panic.

"That's it. Hold on to me."

"Yield, Sabine, and take your pleasure."

They began to move, thrusting in perfect rhythm. A cry started low in my throat as I rocked between them.

"Too much?" one murmured. Maddox. I gripped him closer.

"Please. Faster, harder."

They obliged and I lost myself in their movements, and drowned in the overwhelming joy I felt in the bond. I was myself and not myself, a rushing tributary into a greater ocean made up of our three souls.

You will not lose yourself, they told me. *We will not allow it. You are Sabine, and you are ours.*

Say our names, Ragnvald ordered.

I gasped, unable to find my voice.

Maddox surged up and kissed me, and I tasted my own tears.

Not like that, little witch. Speak to us from the heart.

I found the path between us and whispered mind to mind, *Maddox. Ragnvald.*

Again. Back on earth, they sped their thrusts into my body, and the sensation that had built between us threatened to shatter us into little pieces. I whispered their names over and over, a litany that held me together.

Maddox. Ragnvald.

Mine, the warriors answered, and sank their teeth into my neck. I cried out in happiness, and pleasure exploded in the bond, each achingly perfect moment followed by another, stars in a vast constellation spanning over a new world, a place where I could live forever, with my men.

∼

"You knew this would happen," I whispered to Maddox, much, much later, as we lay in each other's arms. "You knew if you took me, I'd fall in love with you. Admit it, wolf."

He took my hand and laid over his heart. "Shhh. Rest now, little witch. We'll argue about it in the morning."

I fell asleep with his fingers curled inside me.

∼

A MOON LATER, I stood on the threshold of my new home, built from massive logs hewn by Berserker hands.

"And here is the bed," Maddox said, leading past the giant stone hearth that made up half of one wall. "We built it ourselves. None of the pack will ever touch it."

A great tree stood in the center of the lodge. Careful hands had carved a headboard out of the living trunk, and the branches made a canopy. I traced the runes scribed into the bark.

"Does this suit you, little witch?"

Unable to speak, I nodded.

"Then we will leave you to enjoy your new home," Ragnvald said, and he and his warrior brother exchanged a grin.

Once I'd shown them out, I shut the heavy door--made of logs twice as long and thrice as tall as I was. Leaning against it, I waited.

The knock came a few seconds later, and sounded so loud, it shook my body where I'd pressed against the wood.

With a smile, I opened the door for my two warriors and swept a hand out to invite them inside.

THE END

The Berserker Saga continues with Given to the Berserkers, Muriel's story.

FREE BOOK

Get a secret Berserker book, Bred by the Berserkers (only to the awesomesauce fans on Lee's email list)
Go here to get started... https://geni.us/BredBerserker

A NOTE FROM LEE SAVINO

Hey there. It's me, Lee Savino, your fearless author of smexy, smexy romance (smart + sexy). I'm glad you read this book. If you're like me, you're wondering what to read next. Let me help you out...

If you haven't visited my website...seriously, go sign up for the free Berserker book. It puts you on my awesome sauce email list and I send out stuff all the time via email that you can't get anywhere else. ;) leesavino.com

And if you want more Berserkers, turn the page for the whole list...

WANT MORE BERSERKERS?

These fierce warriors will stop at nothing to claim their mates...

The Berserker Saga

Sold to the Berserkers - – Brenna, Samuel & Daegan
Mated to the Berserkers - – Brenna, Samuel & Daegan
Bred by the Berserkers (FREE novella only available at www.leesavino.com) - – Brenna, Samuel & Daegan
Taken by the Berserkers – Sabine, Ragnvald & Maddox
Given to the Berserkers – Muriel and her mates
Claimed by the Berserkers – Fleur and her mates

Berserker Brides

Rescued by the Berserker – Hazel & Knut
Captured by the Berserkers – Willow, Leif & Brokk
Kidnapped by the Berserkers – Sage, Thorbjorn & Rolf
Bonded to the Berserkers – Laurel, Haakon & Ulf

Berserker Babies – the sisters Brenna, Sabine, Muriel, Fleur and their mates
Night of the Berserkers – the witch Yseult's story
Owned by the Berserkers – Fern, Dagg & Svein
Tamed by the Berserkers — Sorrel, Thorsteinn & Vik
Mastered by the Berserkers — Juliet, Jarl & Fenrir

Berserker Warriors

Ægir (formerly titled The Sea Wolf)
Siebold

ALSO BY LEE SAVINO

Ménage Sci Fi Romance

Draekons (Dragons in Exile) with Lili Zander (ménage alien dragons)

Crashed spaceship. Prison planet. Two big, hulking, bronzed aliens who turn into dragons. The best part? The dragons insist I'm their mate.

Paranormal romance

Bad Boy Alphas with Renee Rose (bad boy werewolves)

Never ever date a werewolf.

Sci fi romance

Draekon Rebel Force with Lili Zander

Start with Draekon Warrior

Tsenturion Warriors with Golden Angel

Start with Alien Captive

Contemporary Romance

Royal Bad Boy

I'm not falling in love with my arrogant, annoying, sex god boss. Nope. No way.

Royally Fake Fiancé

The Duke of New Arcadia has an image problem only a fiancé can fix.

And I'm the lucky lady he's chosen to play Cinderella.

Beauty & The Lumberjacks

After this logging season, I'm giving up sex. For...reasons.

Her Marine Daddy

My hot Marine hero wants me to call him daddy...

Her Dueling Daddies

Two daddies are better than one.

Innocence: dark mafia romance with Stasia Black

I'm the king of the criminal underworld. I always get what I want. And she is my obsession.

Beauty's Beast: a dark romance with Stasia Black

Years ago, Daphne's father stole from me. Now it's time for her to pay her family's debt...with her body.

ABOUT THE AUTHOR

Lee Savino is a USA today bestselling author. She's also a mom and a choco-holic. She's written a bunch of books—all of them are "smexy" romance. Smexy, as in "smart and sexy."

She hopes you liked this book.

Find her at:
www.leesavino.com

Text copyright © 2015 Lee Savino
All Rights Reserved

No part of this book may be reproduced in any form or by any electronic or mechanical means including information storage and retrieval systems, without permission in writing from the author. The only exception is by a reviewer, who may quote short excerpts in a review.

This book is a work of fiction. Names, characters, places, and incidents either are products of the author's imagination or are used fictitiously. Any resemblance to actual persons, living or dead, events, or locales is entirely coincidental.